THE GUNSMITH

475

Six Deadly Guns

THE GUNSMITH

475

Six Deadly Guns

J. R. Roberts

SPEAKING VOLUMES, LLC
NAPLES, FLORIDA
2022

Six Deadly Guns

ISBN 978-1-64540-600-6

Chapter One

Austin, Tx

John Israel, the Governor of Texas, looked up from his desk as the door to his office opened. He sat back, touched his dark beard.

"Good-morning, Governor," he said to Edmund G. Ross, Governor of the New Mexico Territory.

"Governor," Ross said. "Thank you for seeing me."

"Please, sit," Israel said.

The older, grey-haired man sat across from him.

"What can I do for you this morning, Governor?" Israel asked.

"I just heard from my marshals," Ross said. "They can't find hide-nor-hair of The Six. How about your people?"

"I've heard from my marshals and the Texas Rangers," Israel said. "Nothing."

"What about the Pinkertons?"

"Also nothing."

Governor Ross flopped his arms and sat back in his chair.

"Do you know how many people they've killed?" he asked. "Not only men, but women and children. They've got to be stopped."

"That's why I have a suggestion," Governor Israel said.

"What's that?"

"We need a certain kind of man to find these fiends and bring them to justice."

"I want them killed!" Ross hissed.

"Well, that may happen," Governor Israel said, "but mainly we want the raids, and the killings stopped."

"So, what do you have in mind?" Governor Ross asked. "Somebody like Marshal Custis Long?"

"No, his badge will limit what he can do."

"Talbot Roper, then?"

"He's a detective," Israel said. "That's not what we need, either."

"James West, then."

"He's Secret Service," Israel said. "We'd have to go through Washington. It would take forever."

"Well, unless you're talking about Wyatt Earp or Bat Masterson, I'm stumped."

"They would also adhere to the letter of the law," Israel said. "We need someone who would go beyond that."

"And who is this great savior you're leading up to?" Ross asked.

"Clint Adams," Israel said.

Ross raised his bushy eyebrows in surprise.

"The Gunsmith?"

Israel nodded.

"You think he'd do it?"

"I think we need to ask," Israel said. "We can pay him whatever he wants."

"How are you going to get him here?"

"Captain Parmalee of the Texas Rangers knows him," Israel said. "He'll get him here. The rest will be up to us."

"Us?"

"Well, yeah," Israel said. "I think we should both talk to him. After all, two governors have to be better than one, don't you think?"

"If you say so, Governor," Ross said. "When are we doing this?"

"I'll let you know as soon as I hear from Parmalee," Israel said.

Ross stood up and said, "I'll be waiting."

***

After Governor Ross left Governor Israel's office, he called his adjutant in.

"Yes, Sir?"

"Get this telegram off to Captain Parmalee," Israel said. The telegram had already been written, in anticipation of Governor Ross' agreement to the plan.

"Yes Sir."

"I want to see the reply as soon as it comes in," Israel said. "Day or night."

"Uh, and if you're asleep, Sir?"

"Day or night means day or night," Israel said. "If I'm asleep, wake me up!"

"Yessir!"

"Now get out!"

"Yessir!"

As the adjutant left the Governor stood up, walked to a sidebar and poured himself a shot of whiskey. He was disappointed in his Texas Rangers, but at least Parmalee should be able to get to the Gunsmith. Then it would be up to Israel and Ross to convince the man to take the assignment. The Six had to be brought to justice, and it was going to take a man who was just like them to do it.

Chapter Two

Clint entered the Austin, Texas office of Texas Ranger Captain Edward Parmalee. The tall, broad-shouldered man stood up and came around his desk with his hand out.

"Clint Adams," he said, "sonofabitch, how are you?"

"I'm good, Captain," Clint said, as they shook hands. "How are you?"

"Fine, fine," Parmalee said, "have a seat. And thanks for coming so quickly."

"It's not often I'm invited to visit the headquarters of the Texas Rangers, Captain," Clint said. "You went to the trouble of tracking me down, so I figured I'd find out what the story was."

Parmalee went back around behind his desk and sat down.

"Clint, the Governor asked me to contact you on his behalf," Parmalee said. "Actually, his and the Governor of New Mexico."

"New Mexico?" Clint asked. "What's this about, Ed?"

"It's about The Six," Parmalee said. "Have you heard of them?"

"The Six?" Clint asked. "I don't think so. Has it been in the newspapers?"

"No, actually it's only law enforcement that's been calling them that," Parmalee said. "They're six gunmen who have been wreaking havoc in Texas and New Mexico. They've killed men, women and children during raids on towns, during which they've been robbing banks, stages, payrolls, trains . . . whatever they can get their hands on."

"And this hasn't been in the newspapers?"

"The raids and robberies, yes," Parmalee said, "but not the name 'The Six,' and not that the jobs are connected. But they are."

"Well, your men are on it, right?"

"My men, marshals, sheriffs, Pinkertons . . . we've tried everything. Nobody's been able to catch them."

"So where do I come in?"

Parmalee waved a hand and said, "I'm not trying to recruit you, but the two governors would like to talk to you. They'd like you to go to Governor Israel's office, while you're here in Austin."

"So they're going to try to recruit me to track down this 'Six?'"

"I'm actually not supposed to discuss this with you," Parmalee said, "but since we're friends . . . yeah, they're going to ask you to track them down."

"Ed," Clint said, "I don't know—"

"Look," Parmalee said, "just meet with them, don't tell them I told you. Listen to what they have to say and make up your mind."

"Are they going to want to deputize me, or something? I don't want to wear a badge, not even a Texas Ranger—"

"They don't want a lawman, Clint," Parmalee said. "They don't want to handcuff you that way."

"Wait," Clint said, "do they want me to catch these guys, or kill them?"

Parmalee squirmed in his seat.

"I'm getting in too deep here," he said. "They just want them stopped."

"When do they expect me?"

"If you agree to see them," Parmalee said, "it would be tomorrow morning in Governor Israel's office. Governor Ross will also be there."

"Two governors, huh?" Clint said. "I've been in an office with the President, but never with two governors."

"Can I send Governor Israel a message saying you'll be there?"

"Are you in trouble if I don't do this?"

"I'm probably in trouble even if you do," he answered. "I've said too much."

"You saved my life in the war, Ed," Clint said. "I'm not going to give you up."

"I thought you saved my life," Parmalee said.

Clint stood up.

"Oh, is that how it went?"

"Clint—"

"Tell them I'll be there," Clint said.

"Great!"

"After breakfast."

"Uh, right."

"And I'm going to get a room in the best hotel in town," Clint said. "In Texas, right?"

"Definitely."

Clint headed for the door, then stopped and turned.

"Where can I get the best steak in town?" he asked.

"Just by coincidence," Parmalee said, "at the best hotel in town."

Clint nodded.

"Well, that works," Clint said. "Let's have a drink before I leave Austin."

"For sure, Clint," Parmalee said. "That's for sure."

Clint tossed his old friend a wave and left the office.

Chapter Three

"Are you sure he's coming?" Governor Ross asked Governor Israel.

"According to Parmalee he is."

"When?"

"He said after breakfast."

"So what time does he eat breakfast?" Ross asked, checking his pocket watch. "It's after nine."

"I don't know, Governor," Israel said. "We're just going to have to wait."

"We've been waiting," Ross muttered.

There was a knock on the door and Governor Israel's adjutant came in.

"Governor," he said, "Clint Adams is here."

"Finally!" Ross said.

"Governor," Israel said, "I think you better let me do the talking. Show him in, Andrew."

"Yessir."

***

Clint figured by nine o'clock he'd kept the two governors waiting long enough. He presented himself at the state's capital building and was shown into the governor's office by a well-dressed young man.

"Mr. Adams," Governor Israel said, expansively. He rose and came around his desk. "Thank you for coming. This is Governor Ross, from the New Mexico Territories."

"Good-morning, Governors," Clint said, shaking hands with both men.

"Please, have a seat," Governor Israel invited. "Can I offer you some coffee?"

"Thank you, no," Clint said, sitting next to the unhappy looking Governor Ross. "I just had breakfast."

"Of course, of course," Israel said, returning to his chair.

"Well, gentlemen," Clint said, "what's this about?"

"It's about saving lives," Governor Ross said.

"Governor . . ." Israel said.

Ross raised his hands and nodded.

"Mr. Adams, are you aware of a group of gunmen called 'The Six'?"

"Vaguely," Clint said, wanting to cover for Captain Parmalee.

"They're a group that has been terrorizing towns and homesteaders in Texas and New Mexico for months."

"Terrorizing?" Governor Ross blurted. "They've been killing people."

"He's right, of course," Israel said. "They've killed not only men, but women and children, as well."

"They've actually left them hanging from rafters, and poles," Ross said.

"For what purpose?" Clint asked.

"As examples, apparently," Israel said. "To make their point that they're . . . invulnerable."

"What steps have you tried so far?" Clint asked.

"Everything," Israel said. "Sheriffs, marshals, Pinkertons, bounty hunters, you name it."

"And what do you think I can do that they can't?" Clint asked.

"Seriously?" Israel said. "I think you can do what none of them could   think like them."

"Like an outlaw?"

"Like somebody outside the law," Israel said. "You won't have any of the limitations men with badges do."

"Are you telling me you want me to kill these men?" Clint asked.

"I do!" Ross said.

"The Governor is upset," Israel said. "We want them stopped, Mr. Adams. Any way you can do it."

"Now for the big question," Clint said.

"You mean, why should you do it?" Israel said.

"Exactly."

"How about because it's the right thing to do?" Ross said. "How about because these monsters have to be stopped? Because women and children are at risk?"

"How about ten thousand dollars?" Governor Israel asked.

Ross looked shocked.

"Who's paying ten thousand dollars?"

Israel looked at Ross.

"Texas will pay five, and New Mexico the other five."

"And where am I supposed to get the money?" Ross asked.

"We can talk about that later," Israel said. "Well, Mr. Adams?"

Clint rubbed his jaw.

"I could certainly use ten thousand dollars," he said, finally. "But I think Governor Ross' reasons carry a little bit more weight."

"Then you'll do it?"

"I'll need to know everything there is to know about these six men."

"Captain Parmalee can fill you in," Governor Israel said. "That is, if he hasn't already."

"All he told me was that you wanted to see me," Clint said. "But I'll be having a drink with him later today."

"Very good," Governor Israel said. "Will you let me know when you're ready to leave town?"

"Yes Sir," Clint said, getting to his feet. "I'll do that. It was good to meet you." He turned. "And you, Governor Ross."

"Yes, yes," Ross said. "We appreciate this, Mr. Adams."

Clint nodded to both men and left the office.

***

After Clint Adams left, Governor Ross looked at Governor Israel and asked, "Where the hell did that come from about ten thousand dollars?"

"We're going to pay him that."

"He said we didn't have to."

"Come on, Governor," Israel said, "you must have some constituents who will donate money to have The Six stopped for good."

"I could probably scare somebody up," Ross said.

"That's exactly how I feel," Governor Israel said. "So I think we better get to it, don't you?"

Ross stood and muttered, "I suppose so."

Chapter Four

Clint decided to have dinner with Captain Parmalee, rather than just a drink. They met in the lobby of the Austin Regal Hotel and went to the dining room.

"How's your room?" Parmalee asked.

"Probably the best room I've ever had," Clint said. "Better than anything in New York, Denver or San Francisco."

"It's probably very impressive."

"You've never seen a room here?"

"Never had a reason to."

"I could show you mine."

"There's no need," Parmalee said. "I don't need to be envious. But I'll have one of their fine steaks here, and you can put it on your tab—I mean, Texas' tab."

"Done," Clint said.

They both ordered a steak dinner with all the trimmings and then some, and while they ate, Clint asked Parmalee about The Six.

"We have two of their names," Parmalee said. "If you could find one of them, he could give you the rest."

"If I find one, won't I find all six?" Clint asked.

"No, that's just it," Parmalee said. "They split up after every job, go their separate ways. Then they get back together, pull another job, and off they go again."

"Okay," Clint said, "what names do we have?"

As they continued to eat, Parmalee said, "The first name we got was Harry Rome."

"Harry?"

"Harold," Parmalee said. "He was recognized on one of their earlier jobs."

"What's his story?"

"Smart, fast gun, probably the one who sets up the jobs," Parmalee said.

"What's he look like?"

"Tall, rangy, forties," Parmalee said. "He's a hard man, Clint."

"Okay," Clint said. "Who else?"

Parmalee washed down a mouthful of steak-and-potatoes with a big swallow of beer.

"The second name is Bax Kingman."

"Wait," Clint said, "I know that name. Baxter Kingman?"

"That's right. Big guy in his fifties—"

"—likes to use a machete to cut people up."

"You got 'im," Parmalee said. "How do you know him?"

"Our paths crossed . . . oh, maybe ten years ago."

"And you both lived through it?"

"Barely."

"Well," Parmalee said, "those are the only two we've been able to identify."

"And the other four?" Clint asked. "Have they always been the same?"

"As far as we know."

"Who did you send out after them?"

"Two of my best men," Parmalee said. "You know them. Chad and Joe."

Clint did know them. They were good men.

"They came back very frustrated," Parmalee said.

They finished their meal, topped it off with pie for dessert.

"All their crimes have been committed in Texas and New Mexico?"

"That's right."

"Maybe it's because that's where they live."

"Is that where you ran across Bax?" Parmalee asked.

"Yes, it was Texas," Clint said.

"Then you already have a leg up on everyone else, Clint," Parmalee said. "When will you be heading out?"

"No time like the present," Clint said. "Tomorrow morning . . . early."

Chapter Five

Harry Rome looked up as two men came into the saloon.

"It's about time," he said. "I've been here for two days."

"We came as soon as we heard from you," Ben Vincent said. "Where's everybody else?"

"Bax is where you'd expect him to be," Harry said.

The other man, who called himself the Utah Kid for some reason, laughed and said, "The whorehouse."

"Right."

"Jesus," Vincent said, "I hope he don't cut up any whores."

"Get yourself some drinks." Harry said.

The two men went to the bar and came back with a beer each. They sat across from Harry. The Oasis Saloon was the smallest saloon in the town of Antioch, Texas. Harry had The Six meet there because Antioch was a nothing town, with no appeal to anyone. The people who still lived there were born there, as he was. Nobody from outside ever settled in Antioch. There was no reason to.

"We're still waiting for Reese and Patch," Harry said, pouring himself another drink from the whiskey bottle on the table.

"What's the job?" Ben Vincent asked.

"You know we don't discuss that until everybody's here."

"So, we just sit here and wait?" the Kid asked.

"That's what I've been doing," Harry said, "sittin' here waitin' for you guys."

"Why do we always have to meet in this town?" the Utah Kid asked.

"Because I say so," Harry said. "When you're dry behind your ears, maybe you can make the rules."

The Kid frowned and felt behind his ears.

"You explain it to him," Harry said to Vincent. "At another table."

"Come on, Kid," Vincent said, and they moved.

Once they were gone, a saloon girl in a purple dress came over and sat down.

"It's been a while, Harry," she said.

"Hello, Laura."

"How long are you in town for?" she asked.

"A day or two," he said, "no more."

"Got time for me?"

"Maybe," he said. "That all depends. I'll let you know."

"Sure." She stood up and left.

He used to spend a lot of time with Laura, but as he got older, so did she. In her forties now, she had lost much of her appeal.

The Six had been Harry Rome's idea, and for most of the year things had been going fine. He found the five best men he could find, starting with Bax Kingman. Reese and Patch came next, then Ben Vincent and, finally, the Utah Kid. Except for Kingman and his machete, they were all expert gunmen. But it was usually the presence of Bax and his machete that kept them in line.

Harry poured himself another drink, hoped that Reese and Patch would arrive before he got too drunk.

***

The whorehouse was at the very edge of town. In fact, it was outside the town limits.

Baxter Kingman watched as the naked whore approached the bed he was reclining on. He was a huge man in every respect, so he chose the largest girl in the place. She was six feet tall, probably over two hundred pounds, but solid rather than fat. She had long black hair, large, pear-shaped breasts with dark brown nipples, and an unruly thatch of hair between her heavy thighs.

He also saw that she was nervous. Her blues eyes kept going to the machete that Bax never went anywhere without. It was right next to the bed, within easy reach. She knew the big man liked cutting people. She just hoped she could be able to keep him interested in doing other things.

"Come on, girl," he growled at her. "I'm waitin'."

She could see from his huge, throbbing cock that he was ready for her. He smiled broadly as she crawled onto the bed with him and wrapped her hands around his thick penis. It almost burned her, and she could feel it throbbing.

"There ya go, girl," he said. "It's all yours."

He looked down at the top of her head, the smooth, pale skin of her shoulders, as she took him into her hot mouth.

For that moment, the machete was forgotten . . .

***

As it got later and Reese and Patch still hadn't arrived, Harry Rome knew he was going to have to find a way to spend his time. Just sitting there drinking wasn't going to do it.

He looked over at Laura, who at that moment was just standing at the bar. Maybe he was going to have to make time for her after all.

Chapter Six

Clint told Parmalee he wanted to see the Governor again, early in the morning, before he left Austin. Parmalee assured him the Governor would be waiting.

Clint entered Governor John Israel's office at eight a.m. the following morning.

"Governor Ross won't be joining us?" he asked, looking at the empty chairs.

"Governor Ross left for New Mexico after our meeting yesterday. Please, have a seat. Can I offer you coffee?"

"I won't be here that long," Clint said. "I just wanted to cover a few more points before I leave Austin."

"Of course," Israel said. He folded his hands and set them atop his desk. "What's on your mind?"

"I need something that confirms I'm acting for both Texas and the New Mexico Territory."

"I thought you said you didn't want a badge, or anything official."

"Not a badge," Clint said, "but a letter will do. Preferably signed by both governors."

Israel opened his top drawer and took out a piece of paper.

"Do you mean something like this?" he asked, holding it out.

Clint took the paper and read it. It explained that Clint Adams was acting with the authority of Governor Israel of Texas, and Governor Ross of New Mexico.

"You already had this letter ready yesterday?" Clint asked.

"I did," Israel said, "but you didn't ask for it."

"Does this also give me the authority to call in the U.S. marshals, if I need them?"

"It does," Israel said.

Clint folded the letter and stashed it in his shirt pocket.

"Is there anything else, Mr. Adams?" the Governor asked.

"Not really," Clint said, standing. "I just wanted to know the extent of my authority."

"We could still make it even more official," Israel offered.

"That won't be necessary," Clint said, touching the letter in his pocket. "This will do nicely. I'll be in touch."

"Any telegrams you send will be brought to me within minutes," the Governor said.

"I'll try to get you something quickly."

"Good luck," Israel asked.

Clint left the capital building.

***

When he got outside, he found Captain Parmalee waiting by his Tobiano.

"Just came to see you off."

Clint thought it was more likely Parmalee was there to see the Governor.

"Decent of you."

"Where are you headed first?" Parmalee asked.

"I'm going to start looking for Baxter Kingman."

"The man with the machete?"

Clint nodded.

"Will he remember you?"

"Probably."

"Will he try to kill you on sight?"

Clint smiled and said, "Probably."

"Well," the Texas Ranger said, "I wish you luck."

Clint mounted Toby and headed out of Austin.

***

After Clint left, Captain Parmalee went up to the Governor's office.

"Have a seat, Captain," Israel said.

"Thank you, Sir."

"Did you see Mr. Adams before he left?"

"Yes, Sir," Parmalee said. "Downstairs."

"What do you think?"

"About what, Sir?"

"Is he the man for the job."

"Considering you've tried everything else, Sir," Parmalee said, "I'd say there's nobody else."

"I don't want you to tell me he's the man because we don't have anybody else," Governor Israel said. "I want you to tell me he'll get the job done."

"If anybody can do it, Governor," Parmalee said, "it's Clint Adams."

"Why did you never recruit him into the Rangers?" Israel asked.

"Believe me, Sir, I tried," Parmalee said. "And I know the Pinkertons tried many times. He's just not very good at taking orders. He needs to be on his own."

"Well," Israel said, "where this job is concerned, he's gotten his way."

"Yes Sir," Parmalee said, "he has."

Chapter Seven

The Six sat on their horses on a hill and stared down at their next target.

"Are you sure about this?" Bax Kingman asked Harry Rome.

"I'm always sure, Bax."

"Yeah, but that's the smallest bank I ever saw," Kingman said.

"And in that bank," Harry said, "is the payroll for the biggest oil operation in the county."

The Utah Kid moved his lips and pointed while he counted.

"There's only six buildings in this town," he said.

"Believe me," Harry said, "the money's in there."

"Any law?" Bax asked.

"A sheriff and a deputy," Harry said. "One's an old man, and the other one's even older."

"So, we kill 'em?" Bax asked.

"Oh yeah," Harry said.

They started riding down.

***

The six riders stopped in front of the small building that had a sign over the door that said, BALLARD BANK.

"Is that the name of the town," Reese asked, "or the banker?"

"Who cares," Harry said. "Reese, you stay with the horses."

"Right."

The other five dismounted and approached the bank's front door. The Utah Kid was carrying saddlebags for the cash.

"Patch," Harry said, "stay by the door."

"I'd rather go in—"

"We've been through this before," Harry Rome said. "That black eye-patch makes you too easy to identify. So, stay by the door."

"Right."

Harry, Bax, Ben Vincent and the Utah Kid entered the bank.

The two men there turned and gaped at them.

"Just stand still and you won't be hurt," Harry Rome told them. "Anyone else here?"

"N-no," the older of the two said. "T-this is the whole bank. There's nobody else."

Harry could plainly see there were only the two men and, against the back wall, a safe.

"Open the safe," Harry told them.

"You're gonna be disappointed, Mister," the older man said. "This is a small bank."

"We'll see," Harry said. "Open it."

"But Mister—"

Harry shot the younger man, who slumped to the floor.

"All right, all right!" the other man shouted. "J-just don't shoot me."

"Hurry it up!"

"Yes, yes!" The man—presumably the bank manager—went to the safe and started to turn the dial. When he pulled on the handle it didn't open.

"What's wrong?" Harry demanded.

"I-I must have done it wrong," the man said. "I'm very nervous."

"Well do it right this time," Harry told him, "or you're dead."

"Yes, all right." He licked his lips and turned the dial again. This time when he pulled on the handle, the door opened.

"Thanks," Harry said, and shot him.

"Kid! The saddlebags. Fill 'em up."

"Right."

Utah went to the safe and started taking out the cash with two hands. Harry went to the front door and opened it.

"Anything?" he asked Patch.

"Not yet, but somebody musta heard the shots."

"We'll know in a few minutes," Harry said.

He closed the door and turned to Ben Vincent.

"Help the kid with the cash."

"Right."

But when Vincent reached the safe Utah stood up and said, "Got it."

"Let's go!" Vincent shouted.

He, the Utah Kid, Bax and Vincent headed for the bank door. As they exited Patch said, "Somebody's comin'."

"How many?" Harry asked.

"One."

"Bax, you're with me," Harry said. "The rest of you get mounted."

Harry and Bax turned to face the approaching man while the others went to their horses.

"He's wearin' a badge," Bax said.

"I see it."

The sunlight glinted off the star the man wore on his chest. It made an excellent target.

Bax drew his machete from his belt.

"I can take him," he said.

"He'll shoot you before you can get within arm's length," Harry said.

As Harry said that, the approaching lawman drew his weapon.

"Stop where you are!" he shouted.

"He's crazy to go against us alone," Harry said.

"He must be sixty years old!" Bax said. "Maybe he wants to die."

"Then I'll give 'im what he wants."

Harry shot the approaching lawman in the chest. The bullet entered his chest and took a chip off the badge as it did. The man fell on his face.

"Come on!" Harry said.

He and Bax ran to their horses, mounted up, and all six men rode out of the tiny town.

Chapter Eight

Wisdom, Tx

The last time Clint had seen Baxter Kingman was in a Texas town called Wisdom. It was small, with two saloons and one hotel. It was also the home of Bax Kingman. Clint was hoping that he would return there between jobs, when he and the other six split up.

After boarding his horse at the livery and getting himself a hotel room, he went to the local sheriff's office. He knocked and entered. The sheriff's desk was off to the right, set against the wall with a gun rack behind it. The man seated at the desk looked at him.

"Stranger in town," the sheriff observed. "I'm Sheriff Daniels. What can I do for you?"

Daniels was in his late fifties, had probably been on the job a long time. His desk was neat and clean, but the rest of the office was covered with dust.

"Sheriff, my name is Clint Adams."

Daniels' eyes went wide.

"The Gunsmith?"

"That's right."

"W-whataya doin' in Wisdom?" Daniels asked. "This is a small town. Nothin' ever happens here."

"I'm looking for one of your citizens," Clint said.

"Who might that be?"

"His name's Baxter Kingman," Clint said.

The sheriff seemed to shudder at the mention of the name.

"That's not someone you want to find," the lawman said.

"Then you know him?"

"I know 'im."

"Is he here?" Clint asked. "In town?"

"Not right now," Daniels said.

"But he does live here, right?"

"At times, he does live here, but not at the moment."

"Do you know where he is right now?"

"No idea."

"When was he last here?"

"Oh, must be a few months ago," the lawman said. "I'm sorry you missed him."

"That's okay," Clint said. "I'll be in town until he comes back."

"B-but, that could be a long time."

"If he's been gone months, I'll bet he'll be back any time. I can wait."

"Whataya want with him?" Sheriff Daniels asked.

"We knew each other years ago," Clint said. "I just want to get reacquainted."

"You were friends?"

Clint laughed.

"We were never friends," he said. "We just knew each other."

"So . . . you'll be stayin'?"

"I've got a hotel room," Clint said. "Does this town have a newspaper?"

"A small one," Daniels said. "Comes out once a week. The office is just down the street. Turn right when you go out the door."

"Thanks."

Clint left the sheriff's office and headed for the newspaper. When he reached it, he saw the name stenciled on the front window. It said *The Wisdom Word.* He opened the door and entered.

The office was quiet, except for the sounds a man was making working on the printing press. When he saw Clint he looked up from what he was doing. His hands and face were smudged with ink.

"This damn thing," he said. "I have to tickle it to get it to work. Thank God I only do one edition a week." He wiped his hands on a dirty rag. "My name's John Berryman. I'm the publisher, editor and reporter for the Word. What can I do for you?"

"I just got to town," Clint said, "and I was wondering if you heard any news?"

"What kind of news are you talking about?"

"Anything having to do with The Six."

Berryman was in his forties, a sturdily built man with dark hair.

"I could use a drink," he said. "How about you?"

"Sounds good."

"Let's go to my office."

Clint followed Berryman to a door and into a small office. There was a desk, a chair, and not much else. The newspaperman sat at his desk, opened a drawer, and took out a bottle and two glasses.

"Have a seat," he said, handing Clint a glass. "But before we talk, you mind tellin' me your name?"

"Not at all," Clint said. "It's Clint Adams."

Berryman almost choked on his whiskey.

"What the hell is the Gunsmith doin' in a little nothin' town like Wisdom?"

"I'm looking for Baxter Kingman."

"Baxter King—whatever for? I thought you said you were interested in The Six?"

"I am."

"Are you telling me that Kingman is one if the Six?"

"You didn't know that?"

"Are you sure?"

"Dead sure."

Berryman frowned.

"Are you thinking about putting that in your paper?"

"Oh sure," Berryman said, "if I want to end up dead."

Chapter Nine

"Do you know the kind of man Baxter Kingman is?" Berryman asked. "Do you know about his machete?"

"I know all about Kingman," Clint told him.

"Does that mean you know 'im personally?"

"We've met."

"Then Gunsmith or not, you know better than to get in his way."

"I never saw a machete that could outdo a gun," Clint said.

"I've seen him do amazing things with that blade," the newspaperman said. "What do you want with him?"

"Well, to start with I want to talk."

"About The Six?" Berryman asked. "You think he's one of them?"

"That's what I think, yes," Clint said. "And I think he comes back here in-between their jobs. I was hoping you'd tell me if there had been a job, lately."

"What makes you think I'd know that?"

"You're a newspaperman," Clint said. "The activities of the Six is news."

Berryman poured himself another drink. When he held the bottle out, Clint shook his head.

"You're correct," the newspaperman said. "I do keep track of the news."

"Then you know when the Six's last job was."

Clint pointed to stacks of newspapers against the wall.

"Yes, I do."

"When did you last read about one of their jobs?" Clint asked.

"Several days ago."

"Days?"

Berryman nodded.

"A very small town in Texas had their bank robbed. Three men were killed including the local sheriff.

"How many men robbed that bank?"

"The stories I read said six."

"So Kingman may well be on his way back here."

"Maybe."

"Does he have family here? Or a woman?"

"No family," Berryman said, "but he does have a woman."

"Who?"

"Her name's Lily. She works at the saloon."

"Which saloon?"

"We only have two," he said. "She's in the Battle-ground Saloon."

"I'll have a beer there," Clint said, "Care to join me?"

"That depends," Berryman said. "What is the chance of an interview while you're here?"

Clint smiled.

"None."

"Well, go on ahead, then," Berryman said. "Have a beer. Just remember she's Kingman's woman."

"I'll keep that in mind. Thanks for your time."

As Clint left, Berryman was going back to his printing press.

***

The Battleground was small and sleepy. Both the bartender and the lone saloon girl sitting at a table playing solitaire looked bored.

The bartender perked up as Clint approached.

"Beer," Clint said.

"Comin' up."

As the bartender set it down Clint asked, "Is that Lily?"

"Well, yeah, but—"

Clint didn't wait for him to warn him that she was somebody's girl. He picked up his beer and walked to the table.

"Red Queen on Black King," he said.

She looked up at him, set the card down and said, "Thanks."

"Mind if I sit?" he asked.

"Help yourself."

As he sat across from her, he studied her. She had black hair, shot with grey, so he put her age somewhere near forty. Even seated he could tell she was a tall, sturdily built woman, the kind a man like Baxter Kingman would go for.

"Can I buy you a drink?" he asked. "You look so bored."

She waved at the bartender, and he brought her a glass of what looked like champagne.

"It's always quiet around here," she said, dealing out a new game.

"Nobody interesting ever comes to town?" he asked.

She looked across the table at him.

"You look interestin'," she said. "Are you gonna be here a while?"

"A few days, at least," he said. "I'm at the hotel."

"Well, then," she said, setting a black five on a red six, "maybe things are pickin' up."

Chapter Ten

After a few more hands of solitaire, Clint and Lily switched to poker. The bartender provided them each with a handful of lucifer matches.

"You must have some customers you look forward to seeing," Clint said.

"Not really," she said, "but maybe you can fill that spot."

"I was warned to stay away from you."

"Now who would do that?" she asked.

"A man named Berryman," Clint said. "The newspaper editor."

"Oh, him," she said, laughing "Maybe that's because I've turned him away more than once."

"He said something about a man named Baxter Kingman."

Lily put her cards on the table, face down, and looked directly at Clint.

"Kingman's a dangerous man," she said. "Everybody stays away from him."

"Does that include you?"

"Yes," she said, "but he doesn't stay away from me."

"Does he think you're his woman?"

"He acts that way."

"Are you afraid of him?"

"You bet I am," she said. "He's crazy, and he always has that machete." She pushed her cards away. "Did you come here lookin' for him?"

"No," Clint said, "I know he's not in town right now."

"But you did come to town lookin' for him."

"Yes, I did," Clint said. "I met him some years ago, and I need to talk to him. I knew this was his home, so I hoped to find him here."

"Well," she said, "if you stay long enough, you will find him. Or, I should say, he'll find you." She stood up.

"Are we finished playing cards?" he asked.

"Playing cards, and talking," she said. "But come around again, Mister . . ."

"Adams," he said, "Clint Adams."

"*The* Clint Adams?" she asked. "The Gunsmith?"

"That's right."

"Well," she said, "then maybe you better come back later tonight, and we can talk some more. I might have somethin' to tell you about Baxter Kingman."

"I'll be here," Clint promised.

Lily smiled at him and walked away. He watched her as she went up the stairs to the second floor, then he turned and walked out of the saloon.

***

After Clint Adams left the saloon Lily came back down with a shawl over her bare shoulders, and also left the saloon. She went directly to the sheriff's office.

"This is a surprise," Sheriff Daniels said when he saw her. To what do I owe this pleasure?"

"You know Clint Adams is in town?"

"I do," Daniels said. "He came to see me."

"Well, he came to see me, too," she said. "Was it about the same thing?"

"Bax Kingman," Sheriff Daniels said.

"So, he's after Bax," she said. "We have to warn him."

"You'd have a better chance of doin' that than I would," Daniels said. "I don't know where he is or how to contact him."

"I don't know why I came here," she said. "You're no help."

"I'm the law, Lily," he said. "Baxter's an outlaw."

"He lives here, Sheriff," she said. "He's one of us. We can't stand by while the Gunsmith kills him."

"You know," he said, "of the two of us, you'd have a better chance of distracting Adams than I would."

"And that's probably what I'm gonna have to do," she said. "Only I don't want Bax to kill Adams, either."

***

Clint spent the remainder of the afternoon and early evening reading in his room—a book of poetry by Ralph Waldo Emerson. He was trying to read poetry of late but was having trouble with it. After a while he quit trying and went out to find someplace to have supper.

When he got to the lobby, he decided to ask the desk clerk where to eat.

"We have a small dining room that's pretty good," the man said. "Other than that, there's a small café a few streets down, or you could get something at the saloon."

"Can your dining room do a steak dinner?"

"They sure can."

"I'll go there, then."

"Through that door," the clerk said, pointing.

Clint had seen the door when he first checked in, but assumed it led to a closet. He walked to it, opened it and saw a small dining room, with six tables, all empty at the moment.

A lonely looking waiter turned and looked at him in surprise. He was about sixty, a small, thin man with a white apron around his waist. When he smiled, he looked genuinely happy to see Clint.

"Can I help you, Sir?" he asked. "A table?"

"Please."

"Help yourself."

The place was so small that any table gave full view of the room and the door, so Clint simply sat at the first table.

"You're a guest?" the waiter asked.

"I am."

"Welcome," the waiter said. "My name's Andy. What can I get you, Sir?"

"The clerk told me you could do a steak dinner."

"Oh yes, Sir," Andy said, "with all the trimmings."

"Then that's what I'll have," Clint said, "and a beer."

"Coming up, Sir."

Andy brought the beer in a large, cold mug, then followed with a platter that contained a huge steak surrounded by three different kinds of vegetables. When Clint cut into the steak, it bled exactly the right amount.

"Is it all right, Sir?" Andy asked.

"It's perfect, Andy," Clint said. "It's about as perfect a steak as I've ever seen."

"That's great!" Andy said. "I'll let the cook know."

"You do that."

Andy returned to the kitchen happily, and Clint put all his attention on his plate.

Chapter Eleven

Clint finished his surprisingly good steak. When he had seen the size of the dining room, he didn't expect much, but the cook knew exactly what he was doing.

"Anythin' else, Sir?" the waiter asked.

"No, thanks," Clint said, "that was perfect."

"You think that was good, come back for breakfast," Andy said.

"I just might do that."

He paid his bill and left the dining room and the hotel.

***

As he entered the Battleground Saloon, it was three times as crowded as it had been the first time he was there. That meant there were three customers. But he didn't see Lily.

He went to the bar and ordered a beer.

"Is Lily working tonight?" he asked as the man set the beer down.

"She should be down soon," he said, "But if you're Clint Adams, she said you should go right up."

"She did, huh?"

"Yep."

"What room?"

"Four."

"Let me have a glass of champagne."

Clint picked up the beer and champagne, walked across the floor to the stairs. He walked down the hall to room four and knocked.

"Who is it?"

"Clint Adams."

"Come on in."

"My hands are full."

He heard her steps and then the door opened. She was wearing a glittery red gown, her shoulders exposed, which he assumed was for her night shift.

He held out the champagne to her.

"Thank you," she said, accepting it. "Please, come on in."

Clint entered and closed the door behind him. Lily carried her glass to a dressing table and sat in front of the mirror. She started to tend to her face, which looked perfect the way it was to Clint.

"You said this afternoon you might have more to say about Baxter Kingman," he reminded her.

"That's right, I did," she said. She turned so she could look directly at him. "I would like for you not to kill him."

Clint took a sip of beer before he replied.

"What makes you think I want to kill him?"

"Well," she said, "you're the Gunsmith. Isn't that what you do?"

"Not without reason," he said. "Will Kingman give me a reason?"

"Probably," she said. "He likes hurting people."

"And killing."

"Yes."

"Does that appeal to you?" Clint asked. "Is that why you're his woman?"

She smiled.

"I'm not his woman," she said. "He just thinks I am."

"Then why would you plead with me not to kill him?" Clint asked.

"He's from here," she said. "He's local, and this is a small town. We look out for each other."

"Tell me," he said, "are you afraid of him?"

"Oh yes," she said, "definitely. But that doesn't mean I want him dead."

"Would you be happy if he never came back here?" Clint asked.

"Very," she said. "But right now, I'm happy that you're here."

She walked up to him, took the beer from his hand, set it aside, and kissed him.

Chapter Twelve

They kissed for a while and then it seemed as if they were suddenly naked on the bed, together. She was solidly built, without an ounce of fat. She had large breasts, wide hips and lovely, smooth skin. If she was in her forties, she was certainly wearing the years well.

They pressed their bodies together, his erection pinned between them. She was a strong woman and used her strength to flip him onto his back. Then she shimmied down his body until her face was between his legs. He turned his head and saw his gun on the table next to the bed, within easy reach, but he didn't recall having put it there. Then she took his cock into her mouth and he reached to cup her head in his hands and stared at the ceiling as she worked him into a tremendous explosion . . .

***

Later, she was on all fours, presenting her majestic butt to him.

"There it is," she said, "All yours. Do what you want with it."

He leaned over, kissed each cheek lovingly, then ran his tongue between them for a while. She gasped and moaned but caught her breath completely when he got to his knees, spread her cheeks and drove his cock into her.

"Oh, Jesus!" she cried.

"Hey," he said, "you asked for it."

"I'm . . . not . . . complaining," she gasped, as he lunged in and out.

To illustrate her point, she started pushing back at him every time he slammed into her, so the room filled with the sound of flesh slapping flesh.

He was on the verge of finishing, when he withdrew, turned her over into her back, and drove himself into her hot pussy.

"Oh, yeah," she groaned, "oh, yes . . . oh . . . oh . . . oh, my!"

Her entire body trembled and at that moment he released a torrent of hot semen that made her eyes go wide, and then oddly vacant . . .

***

"So tell me," Clint said, as they lay side-by-side, "when was the last time you saw Baxter?"

"The last time he was here," she said.

"And when was that?" he asked. "I don't remember if you told me."

"It was . . . weeks ago," she said.

"And when he comes home, how long does he usually stay?"

"That depends, I guess," she said. "Days, sometimes weeks."

"Has he ever stayed longer?"

She thought a moment, then said, "Maybe once or twice."

"But he has stayed for months?"

"He has," she said, "but not recently. Lately, he stays for a few weeks, then goes."

"And," he asked, "when he comes, do you and he ever spend time here?"

"In the saloon, yes," she said, "but in bed, no, never."

"Never?"

"No."

"How can he assume you're his woman if you don't spend time in bed?"

"He just wants people to think I'm his," she said.

"And you let them?"

"Yes."

"Why?"

"Like I said before," she answered, "he scares me."

"So if he wanted you to go to bed with him, you would?" he asked.

"Well," she said, turning her head to look at him, "at that point, I'd have to decide just how scared of him I was."

***

When Clint went back down to the saloon there were four customers, not three.

He went to the bar and ordered a beer.

"Comin' up," the bartender said.

When he set the beer in front of Clint, he stood there for a moment.

"What's your name?" Clint asked.

"Homer."

"What's on your mind, Homer?"

"You're lookin' for Baxter Kingman?"

"I am."

"You, uh, understand that he's crazy?" Homer asked.

"I understand that very well."

"And you still want him?"

"I do."

"Are you gonna kill 'im?"

"That's going to be up to him."

"I don't think he'll give you a choice."

"I guess we'll have to see, won't we?"

"Well," Homer said, "I hope you do."

Chapter Thirteen

Harry Rome set the six stacks of cash down on the table in front of him. The front door of the saloon in Antioch, Texas was locked. The bartender behind the bar was satisfied with the six customers he had. They may have been outlaws, but they paid for their drinks.

From his seat at the table Harry Rome looked up at his partners. In return, the five men looked at the stacks of cash.

"Equal split?" Bax asked.

"As usual," Harry said.

Vincent, Reese, Patch and the Utah Kid all nodded.

"All right," Harry Rome said, "take your money and go."

They all picked up a stack of cash.

"When's the next job?" Utah asked.

"I'll let you know," Harry said. "As usual."

"One last drink!" Bax said, and the five of them went to the bar.

When they all had a mug of beer in their hands, Bax walked back to the table and handed one to Harry.

"Have a seat," Harry said.

Bax sat across from him. Harry looked over at the other four and was satisfied that they couldn't hear him.

"You headed home to Wisdom after this?" he asked Bax.

"Unless you can think of some place better to go," Bax said. "You got another job planned?"

"Not yet," Harry said. "I just wanna know where you're gonna be."

"I'll be in Wisdom," Bax said. "I gotta see my woman."

"The folks there know who you are, right?"

"They know," Bax said. "I'm Baxter Kingman, born and raised there."

"That's all they know."

A wolfish grin crossed Bax Kingman's face.

"That's all they wanna know."

"Just so long as I can find you there."

"You'll find me," Bax said, then looked at the bar. "What about them?"

"I'll find them," Harry said. "Probably in the same place, together."

"Ain't we supposed to split up between jobs?"

"Yeah," Harry said, "they think I don't know that they stay together, two and two."

"Reese and Patch?"

"Yeah, and Utah and Ben."

"Where?"

"Patch and Reese go across the border, to a town called Cortez," Rome said. "The Kid and Ben go to Big Bend, New Mexico."

"Why?" Bax asked.

"Well, I guess Patch and Reese think it's safer in Mexico," Rome said, "while the Kid and Ben think Big Bend just the right size for them not to be noticed."

"Yeah, but why stay together?"

"Who knows?" Harry said. "Maybe so they don't get lonely." He laughed.

Bax looked at the other four again.

"I never trusted them."

"They've done good, so far," Harry said. "When are you headin' for Wisdom?"

"As soon as I finish this beer," Bax said. "I'll see ya, Harry."

He drained the mug, got up and left the saloon.

Harry Rome sat back with his beer and regarded the four men at the bar. It might be time for The Six to import some new blood.

***

So far Wisdom had been a pleasant stop. He'd had a pleasant night with Lily, and he had found a decent place for breakfast. Now it was three days later, and he'd managed to spend one more night with Lily, who still insisted she wasn't Bax Kingman's girl.

On the fourth night he entered the saloon and went to the bar. Homer greeted him with a beer.

"Goin' up to see Lily?" Homer asked.

"Not just yet," Clint said. "I thought I'd hang around down here for a while."

"Still waiting for Bax Kingman to show up?" Homer asked, leaning on the bar.

"Have you seen him?" Clint asked.

"Naw," Homer said, "if I had, I woulda toldja. Remember, I want you to kill 'im."

"Yeah, you said, that," Clint said, "but you never told me why".

"Let's just say I want him to stop comin' here and leave Lily alone."

"Lily sounds protective of him."

"Well, sure she is. They grew up together," he said. "That's the only reason I can think of. Jesus, he tells everybody she's his woman, but she thinks of him as a little brother."

"Really?" Clint asked. "I didn't get that."

"Then don't tell 'er I told you," he said.

"I won't," Clint promised.

He took his beer to one of the empty tables and sat. If Lily thought of Kingman as her "little brother" it might explain a lot. Except that she had told Clint she was afraid of Kingman. Why would she be afraid of her "little brother?"

Clint decided to finish his beer and then see if he could find some information on Lily and Bax elsewhere.

Chapter Fourteen

Clint decided to start with the sheriff.

"What can I do for you, Adams?" Sheriff Daniels asked as Clint entered his office.

"I heard something, and I want to confirm it with you," Clint said.

"What's that?"

"Somebody told me that Lily, over at the saloon, considers Bax Kingman to be like a younger brother. That they grew up together."

"That sounds true," he said.

"Any reason why you didn't tell me that before?" Clint asked.

"You didn't ask," the sheriff said.

"Still," Clint said, "it sounds like something you might've told me."

"I thought I'd leave that to Lily," the sheriff said, "but I guess she didn't tell you either."

"No, she didn't," Clint said. "But everybody else knows, don't they?"

"Pretty much," Daniels said. "Folks around here don't talk to strangers. Who told you?"

"I think I'll keep that to myself," Clint said. "Thanks for your time."

Clint left the sheriff's office and took a moment to decide where to go next. He decided some of the store-keepers might be in the mood to talk, if their businesses were in as bad shape as the saloon's.

He turned out to be right. Most of the stores—the ones that were still open—contained bored clerks who were quite willing to talk about certain things.

In a leather shop the clerk said, "Well, sure, Lily grew up here with Bax Kingman. She stayed, and he comes and goes."

"Do you know where he is when he goes?" Clint asked.

"I know better than to ask 'im," the older man said. "Not while he's got that machete in his belt."

An older woman in a dress shop said, "Ever since he was a boy you could see the bad in Bax Kingman."

Clint asked the middle-aged clerk in the gun shop, "Why do you suppose he keeps coming back here?"

"Well," the man said, "he claims it's his home, the only one he's ever known."

"Keeps calling him back, eh?"

The man nodded.

"Thanks."

Clint left and went back to the saloon.

***

"Beer," Clint told Homer.

"What've you been up to?" the bartender asked, setting the beer down.

"Checking on what you told me about Lily and Kingman," Clint said.

"And?"

"Seems you were telling the truth."

"Why wouldn't I?" Homer asked. "I told you, I want you to kill him."

"I got that feeling from some of the other citizens, as well," Clint said.

"When he comes home, he acts like he owns the place," Homer said.

"Why do you suppose Lily didn't tell me they grew up together?" Clint asked.

"Probably because she didn't want you to know."

"But why?"

Homer shrugged.

"You'll have to ask her that."

"I think I will."

He turned and regarded the room. There were about eight customers present.

"Looks like a rush," he said.

"It's about time," Homer said.

"Regular customers?"

"Pretty much."

"I guess I'll go up and see Lily."

He headed for the stairs, but before he could start his ascent, Lily appeared at the head of the stairs and walked down.

"Waiting for me?" she asked, when she reached the bottom.

"As a matter of fact, I am."

"Let's go to my table."

They walked across the room together and sat. Homer immediately appeared with a glass of champagne for Lily.

"Thank you, Homer," she said.

Homer nodded and returned to the bar.

"You've got something on your mind," she said. "I can tell."

"You think you know me that well after a few days?" he asked.

"Well, enough."

"You're right," he said. "Why didn't you ever tell me that you and Bax Kingman grew up together?"

"Oh," she said, and turned her attention to her champagne.

Chapter Fifteen

"Well?" Clint said. "The way I heard it, you were like brother and sister."

"We still are."

"All the more reason you could've told me."

"You're probably right."

"So?"

"I mostly told you the truth," she said. "Bax does tell people I'm his woman, and I am afraid of him."

"You think he'd hurt you?"

"Oh, not deliberately," she said. "But when he drinks, he gets mean. And he takes out that machete of his."

"I see."

"You probably don't," she said. "But if you stay around here long enough, you will."

"I've seen Bax in action with that machete," Clint said.

"That's right, you said you knew him."

"Kind of," Clint said. "Let's just say our paths have crossed."

"And they're gonna cross again?"

"That's why I'm here."

"You're not gonna kill 'im, are you, Clint?"

"That's not my plan," Clint said.

She finished her champagne and put the glass down.

"Listen, Clint, it may not be your plan, but if you rile 'im, you may have to kill him, or he'll kill you."

"Then I'll try not to rile him," Clint said.

***

As the hour got later, more customers entered. Eventually, there were about twenty men there, most of them hands from a nearby ranch. Lily left Clint at her table while she circulated, working the men. Clint thought she was doing it to avoid talking to him anymore. Maybe she had slept with him two nights, to keep him busy. There might not be a third.

He left the saloon while she was still working the ranch hands, laughing and drinking with them. On the way to the hotel, he heard a familiar sound in the quiet night, a hammer being cocked. It warned him, and he was already moving when the shot was fired. He rolled, took cover behind a horse trough, gun in hand. He waited for a second shot, so that the muzzle flash in the dark would show him where the shooter was. But it never came.

One shot in the quiet town was enough to rouse some attention. A crowd of men came out of the saloon, with

Lily in their midst. Clint was about to walk over when Sheriff Daniels appeared.

"What happened?" he asked.

Clint holstered his gun.

"Somebody took a shot at me."

"Who?"

"If I knew that I wouldn't be standing here."

"You didn't see anybody?"

"No," Clint said. "I heard the hammer being cocked and hit the ground. There wasn't a second shot."

"Somebody must've recognized you," Daniels said.

"Or," he said, "somebody doesn't want me asking any more questions about Bax Kingman."

"You think one of our citizens did this?" Daniels asked. "I don't think so. These are good people."

"I'll bet most of them are, Sheriff," he said.

Clint looked over at the saloon, where the men were filing back inside accompanied by Lily.

"What about Lily?" he asked. "If she considers Baxter Kingman her brother—"

"She'd never do somethin' like this."

"She could have it done."

"She ain't got it in 'er," Daniels insisted, shaking his head.

"Well," Clint said, "somebody does. Does Kingman have any old friends in town?"

"Not really," Daniels said. "Most folks just put up with him because he's a hometown boy, but they ain't his friends."

Clint changed the subject.

"Have you heard anything about The Six pulling a job recently?"

"I heard something about a bank in a small town called Ballard, but don't know if it was them."

"What happened?"

"Two bank employees and a lawman were killed."

"Witnesses?"

"A couple," the sheriff said. "They said there could've been six men, or more."

Clint nodded.

"It was probably them," he said. "They go to ground soon after each job, until they get called together again by the boss, Harry Rome."

"Rome?" Daniels said. "He's the leader of the Six?"

"That's the word we got," Clint said. "Why?"

"I know 'im, is all," Daniels said. "He was here a while back, maybe to recruit Kingman."

"Well," Clint said, "we should know pretty soon if it was The Six, because Kingman will come home."

"And you'll kill 'im?"

"Not my plan," Clint said. "I just want to talk to him."

"You try to talk to him, and either he'll kill you, or you'll kill him."

"I guess we'll find out," Clint said. "Thanks, Sheriff."

Chapter Sixteen

It took two more days of sitting around in front of the hotel, two days that made Clint take up whittling at some point.

Now that he knew Lily's relationship with Bax Kingman a little better, they weren't spending nights together anymore.

Finally, after a week in Wisdom, Kingman came riding down the main street—one of the only streets—big as you please. He made the horse beneath him look like a pony, reminding Clint of how big a man he truly was. And the sun glinted off the metal of the machete in his belt.

Clint remained where he was and watched as the man continued past the hotel without seeming to look around him. But Clint knew, with the business Bax Kingman was in, that he had probably seen him sitting there.

He rode to the livery stable at the end of the street, dismounted and walked the horse into the barn.

Clint tried to decide what to do before Kingman came out again, but in the end figured he would remain where he was and see what Kingman would do.

Kingman came out carrying his saddlebags and rifle. As he walked up the street toward Clint it was clear he wasn't carrying a pistol.

It was no surprise to Clint when Kingman walked right up to him.

"What the hell are you doin' here, Adams?" the big man asked, staring down at Clint.

"I'm just passing through, Kingman," Clint said. "What are you doing here?"

"I live here," Kingman said.

"Is that a fact?" Clint said. "This little town?"

"I grew up in this little town," Kingman said. "It's home, so don't say nothin' bad about it."

"I wouldn't dare," Clint said.

"You stayin' here at the hotel?" Kingman asked.

"That's right," Clint answered. "You?"

"I told you," Kingman said. "I love it here. Just stay out of my way."

Clint eyed the saddlebags over Kingman's broad shoulder. He wondered how much of the bank money was in there?

"See you around," Clint said.

"You better hope not," Kingman said.

Clint watched the big man walk away, kept him in sight as he bypassed the saloon and turned a corner. He realized one of the things he should have done over the past week was find out where Kingman lived. He didn't want to follow the man, the town was too small to be able to do that unnoticed. Instead, he headed for the sheriff's office.

***

Sheriff Daniels was sweeping the floor when Clint entered the office. He stopped, leaned on the broom.

"What can I do for you today, Mr. Adams?" he asked.

"Kingman just rode in."

Daniels put the broom aside.

"Did he see you? Recognize you?"

"Both," Clint said, "and he approached me."

"And?"

"Warned me to stay away from him."

"So what now?"

"I thought you could tell me where Kingman lives," Clint said.

"I wondered why you never asked me that before."

"Yeah," Clint said, "so do I."

"Just south of town his family had a house," Daniels said. "It ain't much, but it's where he stayed whenever he was in town."

"I saw him leave his horse in the livery," Clint said. "Is there no barn where he lives?"

"No," Daniels said, shaking his head, "the barn burned down many years ago."

"How did that happen?"

Daniels grinned.

"When Bax was a boy, he burned it down."

***

Sheriff Daniels told Clint the house was walking distance, so Clint headed out on foot. When he came within sight of the house, he slowed, then took cover behind a thick tree. Moments later Kingman came out the door with a blanket and shook it. Dust flew into the air. He shook it again, then went back inside. That must have been Bax Kingman's version of house cleaning.

Once the big man went back inside, Clint broke from cover and approached the house. He peered in the window, saw Kingman sitting at a table with a bottle of whiskey. His machete was on the table. The big man seemed to be very relaxed. The next moment illustrated that fact when he put his feet up on the table.

Clint decided now was as good a time as any to approach him about The Six.

Chapter Seventeen

Clint slammed the door open, expecting Kingman to drop his feet from the table and stand. Instead, the man just turned his head and looked at Clint.

"I been expectin' you," he said.

"Is that right?"

"You don't think I believe you're here by coincidence, do ya?" He waved with the bottle. "Have a drink."

Clint hesitated, then walked to the table and sat in the chair across from Kingman. The big man reached out, put the bottle on the table, next to the machete. Clint tensed, but Kingman never made a move for the blade.

Clint picked up the bottle and took a drink, then set it back down.

"What's on your mind, Adams?" Kingman asked. "It's been years since we seen each other. I don't remember doin' anythin' that'd bring you after me."

"You've done something, Kingman," Clint said. "A lot of something. You and The Six."

"The Six?" Kingman asked. "You think I'm one of The Six?"

"I know you are," Clint said. "I also know Harry Rome is the leader. What I need to know is, who are the other four and where do I find them?"

Kingman looked at the machete on the table, but when he reached out, it was for the bottle.

"Harry Rome?" he said, after taking a drink.

"Come on, Bax," Clint said. "He was recognized, and you pretty much stand out with that machete."

"Why does it matter to you?"

"Oh, didn't I mention?" Clint asked. "I'm here on behalf of the Governors of Texas and New Mexico. They've asked me to track down The Six. You're the first."

Kingman put the bottle down and looked at the machete.

"Go ahead," Clint said. "Pick it up."

"My machete against your gun?" Kingman asked, withdrawing his hand. "I don't think so."

"Then just tell me who the others are, where I can find them and Harry Rome."

"I never said I knew Harry Rome, or the others," Kingman said. "Or that I'm one of The Six."

"I don't need your confirmation."

"Then I guess you better shoot me," Kingman said, "because I ain't tellin' you nothin'."

Clint looked at the machete, then picked up the bottle of whiskey and took another drink. When he put it back down, he closed his hand over the hilt of the machete.

"Don't!" Kingman said.

Clint looked at Kingman, but kept his hand on the machete.

"Nobody handles my blade," Kingman said.

"Is that right?" Clint asked. "Are you going to stop me?"

"Adams . . ." Kingman said, warningly.

"What will you do if I pick it up?" Clint asked.

"I'll kill you with it," the big man said, then smiled and added, "eventually."

Clint tapped the hilt with his forefinger.

"You won't see it comin'," Kingman told him. "You'll never get your gun out."

Clint closed his hand on the hilt and lifted the machete. Kingman's eyes went cold.

"It's heavier than it looks," Clint said, hefting it.

"That was a mistake, Adams," Kingman said. "A big mistake."

"Give me a name, Bax," Clint said. "One name. I'll find him, and he'll give me the others."

"You already have a name," Kingman said. "Harry Rome, remember?"

"You're not going to give Rome up," Clint said.

"No, I'm not," Kingman said.

"Then give me one of the others."

Kingman thought Clint's request over for a moment.

"Give me some time to think," he finally said.

"Sure," Clint said, "no problem."

He stood up. Kingman didn't move a muscle, but something in his cheek was twitching. He badly wanted to pick up the machete and go at Clint.

"I'll check back with you tomorrow, Bax," Clint said.

"Sure."

"If you're not here, you'll be in the saloon?"

"What makes you ask that?"

"I assume you'll be wanting to see Lily."

Kingman's eyes narrowed.

"What do you know about Lily?"

"We've spent some time together," Clint said. "She warned me about you."

"Warned?"

Clint nodded.

"She said you were violent, and I might have to kill you," Clint said. "She also asked me not to."

"Anythin' else?"

"Not really," Clint said. "Over the past few days, she hasn't had much to say to me."

"That's good," Kingman said. "Yeah, if not here, at the saloon."

Clint nodded and said, "I'll see you tomorrow."

He turned and walked out, half expecting Kingman to lunge at him with his blade.

Chapter Eighteen

The encounter with Baxter Kingman had been interesting. Clint's memory of Kingman was of a much more violent man, who had no self-control. That Kingman would have lunged across the table at him, gun or no gun. Over the years, Kingman seemed to have changed.

Clint looked back at the house. There was no sign of Kingman at the window. He was considering going back inside to see if Kingman had any idea who would have taken a shot at him. But he decided to put that off.

He walked back to town. The street was emptier than usual. Apparently, word had gotten out that Baxter Kingman was home. Clint entered the saloon and approached the bar.

"He's home," Homer said.

"I know," Clint said, "We've talked."

"You didn't kill 'im?"

"I didn't have to."

"Beer?"

"Yeah."

Homer drew the beer and set it on the bar. There was only one other man in the place, sitting at a table, head hanging over his glass. When Homer set the beer down,

Clint noticed that his hand was shaking. The man also looked very nervous.

He turned quickly, drawing his gun. The man who had been sitting with his head down had gotten to his feet and was drawing his gun. Clearly, his intention had been to shoot Clint in the back, so he deserved whatever he got.

Clint fired once, before the man even cleared leather. He fell forward across the table, knocking his beer to the floor.

"I tried to give you a signal," Homer said.

"You were sweating," Clint said. "That was enough."

They both walked to the fallen man, Clint ejecting his spent shell and reloading as he went. He holstered his gun, moved the man's head so they could see his face.

"Know him?" Clint asked.

"I don't *know* him," Homer said, "but I seen him around."

The batwing doors swung inward, and Sheriff Daniels entered.

"What happened now?" he asked.

"This fella tried to shoot me in the back," Clint told him.

Daniels looked at Homer.

"He came in, Sheriff," Homer explained, "and told me to stand behind the bar and not move. When Adams came in, I knew what he was gonna do."

"Did you warn him?"

"I tried," the barman said, "but that fella woulda killed me."

"Do you know his name?" Daniels asked.

"No," Homer said.

"Ever see him in here with somebody else?"

"A time or two," Homer said, "but I really can't remember who."

Daniels looked at Clint.

"You ever see him before?" he asked. "In town or anywhere else?"

"No."

"Do you think Kingman sent him after you?" Sheriff Daniels asked.

"No."

"Why not?"

"First," Clint said, "I don't think he had time. And second, if Bax Kingman wants me dead, he'll come after me himself."

"You're probably right."

"Besides," Clint went on, "the first shot was taken before Kingman even got here."

"That's true." Daniels looked down at the dead man. "All right, it's clear you had no choice. I'll have some men come in and carry him to the undertakers."

"I'm sorry I had to kill him before finding out why he came after me," Clint said. "And if he's the only one."

Clint left the saloon.

***

Clint went back to his hotel room, where he felt fairly sure no one was going to take a shot at him. He decided he needed to finish with Baxter Kingman that night.

It was time for him to move on in his pursuit of the other five members of The Six.

He relaxed in his room until darkness fell, then stood up, strapped on his gun and left. He was going back to the saloon, hoping to find Kingman there.

***

When Baxter Kingman entered the saloon that night, he immediately spotted Lily, sitting at her table. He went to the bar, where Homer wordlessly drew a cold beer and handed it to him. Then he carried it to Lily's table.

"I hear you been busy," he said.

"Sit down, Bax," Lily said, pointing. "We need to have us a talk."

Chapter Nineteen

Kingman sat.

"Yeah, we do," he said. "I heard you been talkin' with the Gunsmith."

"I have," she said. "I've been tryin' to convince him to leave you alone."

"I can do that for myself," he assured her.

"I know you think that, Bax," Lily said, "but you're no match for his gun."

"He won't have a chance to get to his gun."

"Bax—"

"Never mind, Lily," Kingman said. "Either I'm gonna kill 'im, or he's gonna kill me. That's just the way it is."

"Why don't you give him what he wants?" she asked.

"I can't do that," Kingman said. "I can't give up my partner."

"You mean partners, don't you?"

"No," he said, "my partner, Harry Rome. The others don't matter."

"The other members of The Six?"

"What do you know about The Six?" he asked.

"Come on, Bax," she said. "I'm not stupid."

He stared at her, then smiled.

"The Six was my idea, remember?" she asked. "Years ago, when we were kids?"

"I remember," he said. "But it took me and Harry Rome to make it happen."

"So, give Adams the other four, but not Rome."

"I'm thinkin' about it," he said.

She looked past him and said, "Well, you better think fast."

He turned in his seat and saw that Clint Adams had entered. There were eight other men in the saloon, but when they saw that both Kingman and Clint Adams were there, they stood and filed out, quickly. They then turned and started to watch through the batwing doors and through the windows.

Kingman watched Adams walk to the bar and get a beer from Homer.

"What now?" Lily asked.

"Now, we wait," Kingman said.

"Well," she said, "that's a change."

"Oh," Kingman said, "you expect me to run across the floor at him with my machete?"

"The old Bax would've," she said. "I don't know what this new Bax is gonna do."

"The new Bax," Kingman said, "is gonna wait."

***

Clint accepted his beer from Homer, then turned and looked at Lily and Bax Kingman.

"Should I . . . leave?" Homer asked. "Maybe get the sheriff?"

"Don't leave, and don't get the sheriff," Clint said. "Just be a witness."

"Yeah," Homer said, "sure."

Clint nodded, took his beer across the room with him.

"Lily . . ." he said.

"Clint," she said. "You know Bax."

"I do," Clint said. "We talked earlier, but I need to talk to him, again."

"Go ahead," she said, sitting back and crossing her arms beneath her breasts, "talk."

"Whatever you got to say you can say in front of Lily," Kingman said.

"Bax," Clint said, "I need a name. Now, tonight. I'll be leaving in the morning."

"So," Kingman said, "one name."

"That's right."

"And you're not askin' me where Harry Rome is?"

"No," Clint said. "You wouldn't tell me that."

"No, I ain't gonna tell ya."

"Then give me one other name, and where to find him," Clint said.

"I tell ya what," Kingman said, "I'll give ya two names, because you'll find 'em in the same place."

"That's fine."

"Yeah?" Kingman said. "That's all you need from me?"

"Sure."

Kingman looked at Lily, who simply shrugged.

"Do you know the names Patch Pullman and Reese Yates?"

"Never heard of them."

"Well, those are your names," Kingman said.

"And where do I find them?"

"Across the border, in Mexico," Kingman said, "A town called Cortez."

"And why are you telling me this?"

"You asked me to, remember?" Kingman asked. "And I told you I'd think about it. And, Lily likes you."

"I see."

"Okay, well, Bax," Clint said, "I've got to take you in, now."

"I thought you might say that," the big man said, and then came out of his seat with the speed of a cat, swinging his machete.

Chapter Twenty

Clint was surprised by the man's speed. He drew his gun and brought it up. There was a clang of metal-on-metal as the machete impacted with the barrel of the gun. Kingman was strong enough to drive the gun awry, but Clint managed to hold onto it. As Kingman drew the machete back for another strike, Clint brought the gun up and fired.

At the sound of the shot a short scream came from Lily. The bullet hit Kingman in the chest, staggering him, but he continued to bring the machete to bear. Clint was forced to fire a second time. At the impact of the bullet, Kingman dropped the machete, staggered again, and then sat down in the chair. He stared, his eyes wide open. Clint could see that he was still breathing.

"My God!" Lily screamed. "You said you wouldn't kill him!"

"I said I didn't plan on killing him," Clint replied. "I only wanted to take him in and get him to talk. Besides, look at him. He's still breathing."

It was shallow, but he *was* breathing.

Clint ejected the two spent shells, reloaded his gun, and holstered it. Then he leaned over and picked up the machete. By that time, Sheriff Daniels had entered.

"What now?" he asked.

"I apprehended Bax Kingman as part of The Six," Clint said. "He attacked me with his machete, and I shot him."

"He shot him twice!" Lily said, staring at Kingman.

Daniels bent over to examine Kingman. He saw two bloody holes in his chest.

"I better get the doc," the lawman said. "Before he bleeds out."

"You better take this," Clint said, holding out the machete. "And if you look in his house, I think you'll find his share from the last job."

"I'll check it," Daniels said.

"What do we do for him in the meantime?" Lily asked.

Both Daniels and Clint looked at Kingman, whose pallor had become waxy.

"Why don't you try to stop the bleedin'?" Daniels asked.

Lily jumped up from her seat, shouting at Homer, "Get me a tablecloth!"

***

As Clint and the sheriff entered the man's office Daniels asked, "Did you find out anythin'?"

"I got two names," Clint said, "and a location."

"So you're leavin' tomorrow?"

"I am."

"To go where?"

"That doesn't concern you," Clint said.

"That's fine," Daniels said, "I'm just happy you're movin' on. I don't want anyone else to die here."

"Kingman isn't dead," Clint reminded him.

"Yet," Daniels said.

"He might die," Clint said, "but he's strong as an ox."

"He'll probably die after you leave," Daniels said. "You'll never know."

"If he lives, I expect you to put him in a cell and hold him for me," Clint said. "If he dies, he dies."

"How will you know?"

"I'll check back with you," Clint said.

"We don't have a telegraph."

"I know," Clint said, "I'll come back through here."

"I can hardly wait," Daniels said.

Clint left the office and went to the livery to be sure his Tobiano would be ready by morning.

***

Clint checked with the doctor that night and found that Kingman was still hanging on. From there, he went to the saloon to see Lily.

"Where is she?" he asked Homer.

"In her room," Homer said. "She was . . . upset."

"I'll go and see her."

"That might make her more upset."

"I'll try to make her understand," Clint said.

"Want to take a beer and champagne with you?"

"Sure, why not?" Clint said. "I might as well give her something to throw in my face."

Homer grinned and handed him the drinks, saying, "I was thinking the same thing."

Clint crossed the deserted saloon floor and went up the stairs. He knocked on Lily's door.

"Go away!" she snapped.

"Lily, it's Clint."

She opened the door, took the champagne from his hand and tossed the contents of the glass into his face.

"Go away!" she said, again.

"Is that your final word?"

"Unless you want a face full of beer," she said.

Before he could reply she slammed the door in his face.

He was done in Wisdom.

Chapter Twenty-One

One week later Clint rode into Cortez, Mexico, riding down the main street bold as brass. If there was anyplace the Gunsmith could go unrecognized it was in a small, Mexican town.

He rode to the livery first, made sure the Tobiano was well cared for, then left and walked up the street with his saddlebags and rifle. The Mexicans looked at him because he was a gringo, not because he was the Gunsmith. Of course, this close to the border there was always a chance somebody would recognize him, but he'd deal with that when the time came.

He stopped at the first hotel he came to, which was a combination cantina/hotel. The bartender served drinks and gave out rooms.

"I'll put my gear in my room," Clint said, accepting his key, "and then I'll be ready for something to eat."

"Enchiladas and rice?" the bartender asked.

"That's fine."

"Your meal will be waiting."

Clint went down a long hallway to his room, which was small and cramped, but oddly very clean. There was a window that looked out onto an alley. He didn't like that. He'd have to take steps to be sure it was safe. But that could wait until after he dined. He left his saddlebags and rifle on the bed, made sure the window lock worked, and then left to return to the cantina.

The bartender showed him to a table and two girls came out, carrying trays of food. They were dark-haired and pretty, and looked very much like sisters. In Mexican cantinas, there always seemed to be pretty girls.

They set the platters down in front of him, then stood there and giggled. The bartender came over and shooed them away.

"Those are my daughters," he told Clint.

"They're lovely girls," Clint said.

"If you touch them," the man said, "I will kill you. Understand?"

"Perfectly," Clint said. "I'm not here for the girls."

"What are you here for, Señor?"

Clint spooned enchiladas, rice and beans onto his plate.

"I'm looking for two gringos," Clint said.

"There are many gringos in Cortez, Señor."

"I'm looking for a man with an eye-patch."

"Ah . . ."

"Have you seen such a man?"

"Possibly," the bartender said. "I must . . . think about it."

"Take your time," Clint said. "I'm going to eat this excellent food."

"My daughters cook," the man said and walked away.

Clint figured the bartender knew the man with the patch, and would probably see how much he would pay for his silence. Clint decided to follow the man when he left the cantina and see where he led him.

He turned his attention to his food, assuming the bartender wouldn't leave til closing time.

***

After he paid for his meal, he left the cantina and took up a position across the street to keep watch. As the sun went down, the bartender came out the front door and started walking very purposefully down the street. Since this was the man's town and strange to Clint, he knew he would have to follow carefully.

Clint stayed across the street, lagging just behind the bartender. As he passed people along the way, they paid little attention to him, which he was glad of. It was only when he crossed paths with another gringo that he nodded to him.

The bartender led Clint to a part of town that, in the United States, would be considered to be across the deadline. The street traffic there was more raucous, with a fight here and there. Now when he passed Mexicans or Americans, they scowled at him.

The man stopped in front of a small cantina, brightly lit from the inside. He seemed to hesitate, but he finally went inside. Clint crossed the street in order to peer in the window.

The small interior seemed to be teeming with men, both Mexican and American. He was able to see the bartender moving among them. He eventually stopped and disappeared from sight. Clint assumed the man had found who he was looking for and sat down.

Clint moved to the door, sidestepped to let two burly gringos exit, and then entered the place. He had to shoulder his way to the bar, but the patrons there were used to being jostled, and didn't seem to mind. When he got to the bar, he ordered a beer from the busy bartender, who served it so quickly some of it sloshed over the rim of the glass onto the bar. Clint didn't care. The glass was so dirty he had no intentions of drinking from it anyway. But he lifted it and turned, scanning the room for the bartender from his hotel.

He finally located him, sitting with a man who wore a black eye-patch. Now all he needed was for Patch to lead him to Reese, and he would have taken care of half The Six.

Chapter Twenty-Two

Clint had to admit, he was surprised to find that Bax Kingman had told him the truth about where to find Patch and Reese. He had probably done it because he planned on killing Clint anyway. Lucky for Clint, things had gone differently.

Clint watched as Patch drank his beer and listened to what the bartender had to say. He could have walked over and taken the man right then and there, but it seemed to him the man's next move would have to be to contact his partner, Reese. At that point Clint could take them both.

So he held his beer and watched, and when the bartender stood up, he turned his back and watched in the mirror as the man left.

Patch did not immediately follow. Clint remained where he was, watching as the man finished his beer. When he was done, he stood and headed for the door. Clint gave him a short head start, then put down his untouched beer and followed.

He looked both ways when he walked out the door and caught Patch walking to the right. Clint turned and followed at a safe distance.

Patch led Clint deeper into the primarily lawless part of town, to a two-story building he quickly identified as a whorehouse. There were girls in flimsy dresses on the second-floor balcony, beckoning to men below.

Patch walked right up to the front door and entered. It seemed a certainty that Reese was inside as well. Clint crossed over, looked up at the beckoning women, and went up the steps. When he got to the door, he was blocked by a large black man who stood with his arms crossed.

"Stranger," he said.

"So?"

"Strangers ain't allowed," the man said.

"I just saw a man go in, a man with an eye-patch," Clint said.

"That's because he isn't a stranger."

"And is he here looking for his friend?" Clint asked.

"Could be," the black man said. "You still ain't allowed inside."

"What if I want a girl?"

The man smiled.

"Then go to the other side of town," he said. "There are plenty of girls there."

"Now look," Clint said, "I just want to come in and find two men I've been trailing."

"Are you a bounty hunter?"

Clint's first thought was to say no, but technically speaking, he was the bounty hunter for two governors. Still . . .

"No," he said, "I'm not a bounty hunter. I just need to take Patch and his friend—"

"Reese," the black man said.

"Patch and Reese," Clint said. "I need to bring them in."

"Then you're a lawman?"

"That's closer to what I am," Clint said.

"I tell you what," the black man said, "I don't like Patch and Reese, so I'm gonna let you go in and get 'em."

"I appreciate that."

He stepped aside, but as Clint started to slip by, the man placed a big hand against his chest.

"Just them," the black man said, "nobody else."

"I don't want anyone else."

The black man removed his hand and Clint entered. Then he turned to the man.

"Any idea what room?"

"I think Reese was with Desiree," the man said. "Top of the stairs."

"Thanks."

Clint headed for the steps, passing some of the girls who were hanging all over their customers, and a few girls who were alone.

"Can I help you, handsome?" one blonde asked him.

"Another time," he replied.

He got to the stairs and went up quickly. At the top was a closed door. Behind it he could hear raised voices. They were so loud he was able to open the door without being heard.

". . . my time with Desiree, not yours, Patch."

"Never mind the girl," Patch replied.

When Clint got the door opened enough, he saw the two men, one on the bed naked, the other standing alongside, fully dressed. The naked man was sporting a rather small erection. The rather fleshy, nude brunette on the bed with him was stroking it. Clint decided not to wait and see if it got any bigger.

"Stand very still, Patch," Clint said. "Don't go for that gun."

Patch went stiff. On the bed, Reese looked at Clint, then at his gun on a chair across the room. The girl sat up, showing Clint her full, brown nippled breasts.

"You can go, young lady," Clint said.

She slid off the bed, grabbed a robe and wrapped it around herself.

"I ain't been paid," she said to Clint.

On the chair with the gun Clint saw a man's wallet.

"Take it out of that wallet."

"Hey!" Reese, a painfully skinny man complained. "What if she takes too much?"

"It won't matter," Clint said. "You won't need it where you're going."

Chapter Twenty-Three

After disarming Patch, Clint instructed Reese to get dressed, keeping both men covered while they complied. He had Patch's gunbelt over his shoulder, and Reese's weapon tucked into his belt.

"You wanna tell us what this is all about?" Patch asked.

"Sure," Clint said. "When I put you two into a cell, I'll have three of The Six out of commission."

"The . . . what?" Patch asked. But the look on Reese's face told the true story. Both men were stunned.

"Three?" Reese asked.

"Bax Kingman was the first," Clint said.

"Kingman?" Reese repeated. "But he's—"

"—probably dead," Clint said. "He was in bad shape when I left Wisdom."

"You . . . shot 'im?" Patch asked.

"I did."

Patch and Reese exchanged a look as Reese pulled on his boots.

"Shall we go?" Clint asked.

Reese stood.

"Where?" Patch asked.

"We're going to find the sheriff's office."

"We've been comin' here a long time," Patch said. "I'm not sure the sheriff will let you use his jail."

"You better hope he does."

"Why's that?" Reese asked.

"If he doesn't," Clint said, "I may have no other choice but to kill you both."

***

The sheriff was a man named Cisco. He was middle-aged and had been the law in Cortez for over ten years.

When Clint entered the office with Patch and Reese, Cisco stood and stared at the three of them.

"*Por favor*, what may I do for you gentlemen?" he asked.

"I'm assuming you know who these men are," Clint said.

"I do," the sheriff said. "These gringos have been coming to Cortez for some time."

Clint noticed the sheriff spoke English with very little accent.

"Well, as of now they're my prisoners," Clint said. "I'll be needing to use your cells."

"These men have broken no laws in Cortez, that I know of," Cisco said.

"Perhaps not," Clint said, "but they've broken many laws in the United States. I'm here to bring them back."

"So you are an America lawman?"

"Not exactly."

"I cannot allow you the use of my jail unless I know what your authority is."

"If you'll put these men in a cell," Clint said, "we can discuss that."

"Very well."

Cisco led the two men back to the cell block. Clint watched from the door to make sure the lawman locked the cell.

"Would you like a cup of coffee, Señor . . .?"

"Adams," Clint answered, "Clint Adams."

"Ah," Cisco said, "the American legend. The Gunsmith. You should have told me that."

"That's not my authority," Clint said, reaching into his pocket. "This is."

He handed the lawman the letter signed by the two governors. The sheriff read it quickly and handed in back.

"The states of Texas and New Mexico are requesting your assistance, Sheriff," Clint said, pocketing the letter.

"And what laws have these men broken?" Cisco asked.

"They are members of a group called The Six."

"*Dios mio*," Cisco breathed. "I have heard of them."

"Yes, they're pretty well known in these parts," Clint said.

"I've heard many lawmen have tried but failed to capture them,"

"Well, I've gotten three of them," Clint said. "Now I'm after the other three. But first I'll have to deliver these to American authorities."

"So you will be leaving town?"

"Yes," Clint said, "and soon."

"*Bien*," Cisco said, "the sooner the better. Those two have made friends here. I would be careful if I was you."

"I always am," Clint said. "I'll need to talk to them before I leave, so I know where their horses are."

"Of course."

Clint entered the cell block. The two prisoners were sitting on their cots and looked up at him.

"I'll need to fetch your horses so we can leave town tomorrow and head back across the border. Once there, I'll turn you over to the authorities and track down the rest. That includes Harry Rome."

"You know about Rome?" Patch asked.

"Yes," Clint said, "everything but where to find him." He pointed a finger. "But you're going to help me with that."

Chapter Twenty-Four

The next morning Clint appeared at the sheriff's office with Patch and Reese's horses in tow. Sheriff Cisco came out to greet him.

"Good-morning, Señor."

"Sheriff," Clint said. "I hope you're not going to tell me my prisoners escaped."

"Hardly, Señor," Cisco said. "They are safely behind bars, awaiting your pleasure."

"You speak English very well, Sheriff," Clint commented.

"I spent many of my youthful years in your country, Señor. Shall I bring the prisoners out?"

"I'll come in and get them," Clint said.

The sheriff opened the door and gestured for Clint to precede him. Clint entered the office, waited for the sheriff to grab the key from the wall, and then followed into the cell block. He saw Patch and Reese sitting on their cots, with trays of a finished breakfast at their feet.

"Stand up!" Clint said. "We're heading out."

The two men stood as Cisco unlocked the door.

"Out!" Clint ordered.

They stepped from the cell and preceded Clint and Cisco into the office.

"Sheriff," Clint said. "Thanks for your help."

"*Vaya con dios, my friend*," Cisco said.

Clint watched as Patch and Reese mounted their horses, then quickly sprang into the Tobiano's saddle.

"At the first sign of trouble," Clint said, "you're both dead."

"Whataya mean?" Patch asked. "You're the Gunsmith. We ain't gonna try to escape."

"You have friends in town," Clint said. "If they try anything, you're dead."

"We ain't in control of that," Reese complained. "If somebody tries somethin' you can't blame us."

"But I will," Clint said. "Now let's move it out. You'll ride ahead of me."

Patch and Reese exchanged a glance, and then started forward. Clint traveled close behind.

***

The first night they camped Clint watched both men as they saw to the horses and built a fire. When it was burning brightly, he tossed them a wrapped package.

"Bacon-and-beans," Clint said. "One of you cook it, the other can see to the coffee."

"We ain't cooks," Patch complained.

"You can do this much," Clint told him.

The two men exchanged a glance.

"Why do you keep doing that?" Clint asked.

"Doin' what?" Patch asked.

"You keep looking at each other," Clint said. "Are you each waiting for the other one to make a move?"

"You told us you'd kill us if we did that," Reese reminded him. "We're not fools."

"That's good," Clint said, sitting back to watch them prepare supper.

Once they were seated around the fire with their plates and cups Clint said, "Now let's talk about Rome."

"What about him?" Patch asked.

"Where can I find him?"

"We don't know," Reese said. "We never know, until we hear from him."

"Okay," Clint said, "what about the other two?"

"What about them?" Patch asked.

"For one thing, what are their names."

Patch and Reese exchanged a glance once again.

"Stop doing that!"

They both turned their heads and looked at him.

"I need names," Clint said. "If I can say at your trials that you gave them to me, it might help you when it comes to sentencing."

The two men continued to eat their supper and did not look at each other.

Clint ate some of his bacon and beans and then said, "Well?"

The two men chewed and swallowed.

"Utah," Reese said.

"Reese!"

"The Utah Kid," Reese went on. "That's what he calls himself."

"And?"

After a moment Patch shook his head and said, "Vincent, Ben Vincent."

"I don't know those names," Clint said. "Where can I find them?"

"Usually," Reese said, "in a small New Mexico town called Big Bend."

"Why there?" Clint asked.

"Who knows?" Patch said, with a shrug. "I've never been there."

Chapter Twenty-Five

In the first two towns they reached, the lawmen refused to take Patch and Reese off Clint's hands, no matter what the letter he carried said.

As they rode out of the second town Patch asked, "What now?"

"We're going to have to find a larger town, where there's a federal marshal."

"What are you thinkin' about?" Patch asked.

"San Antonio."

"That's a long ride," Reese said.

"We'll restock our bacon ad beans at the next town," Clint said.

"How about the makings of some corn bread?" Patch asked. "We won't get any where you're sendin' us."

"I'll see what I can do," Clint said.

***

The next town was a small one called Layton. Clint didn't bother checking with the local law. They stopped just long enough to restock at the mercantile.

When they camped that night they ate bacon, beans and corn bread.

"When we camp," Reese said, "we don't eat like this."

"You mean . . . The Six?"

Reese nodded.

"How much time do you spend together?" Clint asked.

"Not much," Patch said. "Rome calls us together, explains the job, the next day we pull it, and the following day we split up again."

"So how well do you know him?" Clint asked.

"Not well, at all," Patch said. "We know Bax better. By the way, did you actually kill 'im?"

"I shot him," Clint said. "When I left, he was still alive."

"I can't believe it," Reese said. "I thought Bax was . . . unstoppable."

"A gun will always beat a blade," Clint said.

"I guess so," Patch said. "Still . . ."

"Why did Rome choose you two to be part of his Six?" Clint asked.

"We're thieves," Patch said. "That's what we do. We steal."

"And kill," Clint said. "Don't forget that."

"Uh-uh, no," Reese said. "Not us. Rome and Bax, they do the killin'."

"And Utah," Patch said. "Don't forget Utah."

"He's a killer?" Clint asked.

"That kid has killed more men than all of us put together," Patch said. "He's fast with that gun of his."

"He's fast," Clint asked, "or he thinks he's fast?"

"Oh, he's fast," Patch said. "I've seen him gun down three men at one time, and they never cleared leather."

"If you catch up to him," Reese said, "he's gonna try you."

"I'll deal with that when the time comes," Clint said. "You two need to turn in."

After he tied them hand and feet and they settled down to sleep, he cleaned up and sat at the fire with another cup of coffee. He had been getting very little sleep, but the further they got from Cortez, the least likely it seemed they were being followed by friends of Patch and Reese. Still, when he did sleep, he did so lightly. There was a time—when he was riding Duke, and Eclipse—that he could leave it to those horses to alert him. His Tobiano, Toby, was not reliable, yet. Clint was starting to think it might have been a mistake to take on such a young mount, as Toby had just turned four. Duke and Eclipse were not even that young when he first got them.

He finished his coffee and made sure the two outlaws were tightly bound. From all appearances, they were fast asleep. In moments, after laying down himself, he was as fast asleep as he could afford to be.

***

When he awoke, he saw both Patch and Reese staring at him.

"Trying to figure out how to crawl over here to me and get my gun?" he asked.

"Somethin' like that," Patch admitted.

Clint got to his feet.

"I'll make breakfast and then untie you," he told them.

"We're in no hurry," Patch said.

Twenty minutes later they were all seated around the fire eating breakfast.

"You know," Clint said, "the more you tell me about Harry Rome, the more it'll work in your favor."

"What do you wanna know?" Reese asked.

"Is there a town he spends most of his time in?" Clint asked. "A woman he visits?"

"Like we said before," Patch replied, "we don't know him that well. We don't have any idea where he might have a woman."

"But he likes women, doesn't he?"

"Who doesn't?" Reese asked.

"True," Clint said. "It's just that some men, like Bax Kingman, have a woman—a mother, a sister, a lover—they like to spend time with."

"He never talked about any of those with us," Patch assured him. "We've told you all we know."

"All right," Clint said, "then let's talk about the Utah Kid and Ben Vincent."

Chapter Twenty-Six

They made San Antonio three days later. Clint rode directly to the U.S. Marshal's office.

"Let's go," he said. "I'm ready to part company."

"Are you sure?" Patch asked.

"Positive."

They all dismounted, and Clint gestured for them to precede him.

"Don't try anything," he advised them.

They entered the office, which was large, with a stairway leading up to the cell block. There were two desks, with a man seated at each. One man was a young deputy, while the second, larger desk was occupied by the older U.S. Marshal.

Both lawmen looked up at the three men who entered.

"Can we help you gents?" the marshal asked.

"I have two prisoners for your cells, Marshal," Clint said. "My name's Clint Adams and here is my authority."

He handed the marshal the letter signed by the two governors.

"Impressive," the marshal said standing. "Eddie, put these men in a cell."

"Yes, Sir," the younger lawman said. He sprang to his feet, pointed his gun at the two men and said, "Let's go."

"Remember," Patch said, looking at Clint, "you said you'd speak for us at our trial."

"I'll remember."

"What was that about?" the marshal asked.

"Just an agreement we had for them to talk to me about their partners."

The marshal handed the letter back.

"I'm Marshal Ramsey," he said. "Coffee?"

"That'd be great."

"Have a seat."

The marshal walked to a stove against the wall and poured two mugs of coffee.

"It'll have to be black," he said, handing the mug to Clint.

"That's the way I like it."

Marshal Ramsey sat behind his desk.

"Am I sending these men to the Texas capital, or New Mexico?"

"Texas," Clint said. "I'll send a telegram before I leave here. You'll be hearing from a Texas Ranger captain named Parmalee."

"I know Parmalee," Ramsey said. "You see, I was once a Texas Ranger."

"That's quite a coincidence."

"I knew Parmalee before he made captain," Ramsey went on. "Nice to know he's risen to the top."

Clint drank some coffee.

"What's next for you, Mr. Adams?"

"I have to find the other three," Clint said, "and finish my search for The Six."

"Any ideas?"

"These two told me where to find two others," Clint said, "but I still don't know where to find their leader, Harry Rome."

"So, if you find five of the Six, ain't that enough?" Ramsey asked.

"I'm afraid not," Clint said. "I think Rome would just find five more men, and make up a new Six. No, the only easy way to make sure The Six are gone is to catch all six."

"Well," Ramsey said, "I wish you luck."

Clint finished his coffee and set the empty mug down on the marshal's desk. The younger lawman came down the steps and hung the keys to the cells back on the wall peg.

"They're all tucked in, Sir," he said.

"Go make your rounds, Eddie."

"Yes, Sir."

The deputy left, and Clint stood up.

"I'll get a hotel room. But I'll be leaving in the morning." He started for the door. "Can you suggest a place for a good steak?"

"Stay at the Fairview Hotel and eat there. They have a great cook."

"Thanks," Clint said, "I'll do that."

"It's just a few streets north of here."

"Got it," Clint said. "I'll check in with you before I leave town."

Clint left the marshal's office, left the Tobiano in a livery stable and got himself a room at the Fairview, which turned out to be a large, ornately decorated establishment with beautifully appointed rooms. The restaurant, just off the lobby, was also made up of dark wood and leather.

"Are you a guest, Sir?" the waiter asked, as Clint stepped inside.

"I am," Clint said.

"Then come this way and we'll get you seated," the grey-haired man said.

Once Clint was at a table the waiter said, "I'll get you a menu, Sir."

"That won't be necessary," Clint said. "Marshal Ramsey said I could get a steak here."

"Steak it is!" the waiter said. "And all the trimmings."

"As long as there's no bacon," Clint said, "and no beans."

Chapter Twenty-Seven

Marshal Ramsey was right about the steak meal. It was not one of the best Clint had ever had, but far from the worst. And it was much better than the bacon and beans he had been eating on the trail.

After the meal Clint saw that across the lobby was an entrance to the hotel's saloon. He crossed over and entered. It was large and decorated to match the lobby and dining room. There were several men standing at the bar, and a few others sitting at tables. Clint assumed they were all hotel guests. He approached the bar.

"Help you, Sir?" the bartender asked. He was in his thirties, tall and slender, wearing a black vest over a white shirt.

"Beer, please."

"Are you a guest?"

"I am."

"What room?"

"Fifteen."

"Very good, Sir." The bartender drew him a tall beer and set it in front of him.

"Thank you."

Clint picked it up, turned and started to bring it up to his lips, but paused when he saw the woman in the doorway. She was wearing a long, jade green dress, which revealed her creamy shoulders and the upper slopes of her large breasts. She had lustrous black hair that fell to her shoulders. She stood there and looked around the room. Her eyes fell on him but kept moving. Eventually, though, they came back.

She approached the bar and stood next to him.

"I'm sorry, Ma'am," the bartender said, "but unescorted females are not allowed—"

"What makes you think I'm unescorted?" she asked, cutting him off. She turned her head and looked at Clint. "Tell him, darling."

Clint reacted immediately.

"That's right, bartender," he said. "The lady is with me."

She looked at the bartender.

"Red wine, please."

"Coming up."

She turned to Clint again.

"Thank you."

"Since we're together," he said, "don't you think I should know your name?"

"Barbara Latham," she said. "And yours?"

"Clint Adams."

They stopped talking when the bartender brought the wine. He stared at them both for a moment, then walked away.

"Clint Adams," she said, "the Gunsmith?"

"That's me."

"What's the Gunsmith doing in San Antonio?" she asked.

"Just passing through," he said. "I'll be leaving tomorrow."

"That's a shame."

"Why?"

"We won't have time to get to know each other."

"Well," he said, "if we did away with the small talk . . ."

She put her glass down.

"Your room or mine?" she asked.

"Let's do mine," he said.

"Then lead the way."

He led her across the lobby to the stairs, and up to his room.

"Are we going in?" she asked, as they stood in the hall.

"In a minute," he said. "Tell me, when you saw me in the bar did you know who I was?"

"What do you mean?"

"I mean a woman like you has her choice of men," Clint said, "Why me?"

"Can we go inside?"

"Sure, why not?"

They entered the room and Barbara sat on the edge of the bed.

"I have nothing up here to drink," he told her.

"That's all right," she said. "I don't need a drink."

"Then tell me, what do you need?"

"I needed to meet the Gunsmith," she said, "after the desk clerk told me you were here."

"I'll have to talk to him about that."

"Please don't speak harshly to him," she said. "He was only too happy to tell me."

"I'll remember that," Clint said. "So now that you found me, and we're here, what is it I can do for you?"

"Well," she said, "you can start by taking off your pants."

"Are you sure?"

"Oh, yes," she said.

He looked around, grabbed a straight-backed wooden chair and jammed it beneath the doorknob.

"What's that for?"

"Just in case," he said removing his gun belt. He hung it on the bedpost, and then undid his trousers.

Chapter Twenty-Eight

Of course there was always the chance she had lured him up to his room to set him up for something, but he chose to believe otherwise. She was an incredibly beautiful and desirable woman, and he would have hated it if he had to kill her.

She watched him undress, and when he turned to her, naked, she stood and began to disrobe. As she peeled her clothes off, every inch of flesh that came into view was a revelation.

When she was naked, he found himself holding his breath. Her body was shadows and curves, and he almost didn't know where to look first. Finally, he chose her breasts. They were large, dangled and swayed when she moved, due to their heavy underside. They were pear-shaped with dark nipples and wide aureole.

Impatiently, he closed the distance between them and took those breasts in his hands. They were as heavy as they looked. He lovingly held their weight and fondled them.

"You're an amazing woman," he told her.

She laughed.

"Amazing now," she said. "In a few years these will sag, and I'll be fat, but for today—"

"You're beautiful now, and you'll always be."

"You're sweet."

As he pulled her closer to kiss, she got her hands between them to caress his hard cock. He was about to push her back on the bed when he heard a floorboard in the hall creak. He immediately drew his gun from the holster on the bedpost.

"Really?" she said, looking amused. "You still don't trust me?"

"Just being careful," he said, holstering the weapon, again.

"Come here, you," she said. "Let's see if I can't keep your hands busy."

As it turned out, she kept more than just his hands busy. He used his hands and mouth to explore every curve and shadow of her body. He found himself completely enchanted and engrossed by her, and yet, still aware of his surroundings in case of an attack.

As he nestled comfortably between her spread thighs, she sighed as he went to work with his tongue, closing her flesh around his head in a hot embrace.

To thrust his tongue in even deeper, he slid his hands beneath her majestic butt and proceeded to fuck her cunt with his tongue, flicking it in and out of her until she was gushing.

She was still trembling when he mounted her and drove his cock into her hot depths . . .

*****

"Was that what you were after?" he asked, later, as they lay side-by-side.

"Isn't it what you wanted?" she replied.

"Oh yeah," he said, "from the first moment I saw you."

"Then it's the same for me," she said. "Are you leaving town tomorrow?"

"I am."

"So am I."

"Where are you headed?"

"That doesn't matter," she said, reaching a hand out to stroke his right thigh. "All that matters is what's happening tonight."

"I still don't know why you chose me," he said.

"Because I knew sex with you would be without consequence," she said.

"How so?"

"Because in the morning you'll go your way, and I'll go mine, and there won't be any complications."

"Okay," he said, "but that's in the morning, right?"

"Right," she said, closing her hand around his penis, "that's in the morning."

After she stroked him to a throbbing hardness, she rolled on top and took him into her steamy depths . . .

***

In the morning they had breakfast together but did not discuss any part of their future plans. Instead, they talked a bit about their pasts—which, actually, did not reveal very much. By the end of breakfast, she knew what she had known before, that he was the Gunsmith.

He still knew very little about her. She described a variety of jobs to him, from a storekeeper to a saloon girl. But there was not much more than that. She was apparently determined to keep their time together "uncluttered."

After breakfast they parted company in the lobby of the hotel.

"I'll be taking the morning stage," she told him. "I just need to get my bag and check out."

"After I collect my horse from the livery, I'll be on my way."

"See?" she said, with a smile, "like I said. Uncomplicated.

Chapter Twenty-Nine

Big Bend, New Mexico

By the time Clint rode into Big Bend, he was thinking that his disbanding of The Six was going along too easily. He suspected that all the lawmen and detectives who had previously been sent had tried to find the gang at the same time. Clint's success so far was in finding them one or two at a time. First Kingman, then Patch and Reese. Next would be the Utah Kid and Ben Vincent. After them would come the leader, Harry Rome. He would be the hardest one to find, since none of the other five knew where he was.

But first things first. He had to locate the next two. If they were anything like their partners, they'd either be in a saloon or whorehouse.

Big Bend was a small town. The livery was easy to find, run by a middle-aged man whose hands and face bore the scars of the teeth and hooves of many horses.

"How many hotels are there in town?" Clint asked the man.

"Two."

"Which one's the best?"

"One is as bad as the other."

"Take good care of him," Clint said, indicating Toby.

"Don't worry," the hostler said. "I keep this place cleaner than either of the hotels."

"Good to know," Clint said. "Can you tell me who the law is here?"

"Sheriff Lansbury," the man said, "Been the law here for ten years."

"And is he any good?"

"Naw," the hostler said. "But nobody else wants the job."

"And do you know a couple of men called the Utah Kid and Ben Vincent?"

"I don't know nobody," the man said. "Sorry. I gotta get to your horse."

"Sure," Clint said. "Thanks."

Clint left the livery, carrying his rifle and saddlebags. He stopped at the first hotel he came to, saw what the hostler meant. Most of the furniture in the lobby was covered with dust.

He got himself a room, found it as dusty as the lobby. Luckily, the hotel didn't have a dining room. It would have been covered with dust, as well.

Most towns, no matter how run down, had at least one decent place to eat. He decided to take a walk and find it. But along the way he came to the sheriff's office and decided to stop there first.

Clint entered, saw a white-haired man sitting behind a desk, working on a shotgun with a rag.

"Sheriff Lansbury?" he asked.

"That's me," the man said. "Who're you?"

"Clint Adams."

The man paused, then went back to work with the rag.

"What the hell is the Gunsmith doin' in Big Bend?" the lawman said.

"I'm looking for two men," Clint said. "One is named Ben Vincent, the other calls himself the Utah Kid."

"Don't know 'em." The sheriff said.

"And would you tell me if you did?"

The sheriff looked at him for a moment.

"Don't know that, either. Whataya want 'em for? You turned bounty hunter?"

"No."

"Lawman?"

"Not that, either," Clint said. "It's just a job." He decided not to say anything else. "Thanks for your time."

"Hey!" Lansbury said, putting the shotgun down. "When you find 'em you aimin' to kill 'em?"

"That's not my plan."

"How long you gonna be in town?"

"Until I find them," Clint said. "Have a good day."

Clint left the sheriff's office, having found the man as dusty as the rest of the town. There had also been no sign of a deputy.

He decided the town was small enough that he didn't need directions to the saloons or whorehouses. The first saloon he came to was called The Wagon Wheel. He entered, find the fairly large interior pretty empty at that time of the afternoon. Several men looked up at him from their drinks, but since they didn't recognize him, they turned their attention back to drinking.

At the bar the bartender stared at him wordlessly. His expression could only be described as morose.

"Beer," Clint said.

The man nodded, drew the beer and set it in front of Clint. He tossed a nickel on the bar, as a sign on the wall instructed.

"I'm looking for two men," Clint said.

"No men here," the bartender said. "There'll be a girl here tonight, though."

"Then let's say I'm hunting two men."

"Lawman? Or bounty hunter?"

"Neither one."

"Then I'm through guessin'," the bartender said. "Whoever you're lookin' for, I ain't seen 'em."

That was the general attitude Clint encountered until he was approached in the second saloon.

Chapter Thirty

The second saloon was called The Cactus. It was a little busier than the Wagon Wheel, but the general attitude was the same.

"Don't know nobody," the bartender said, serving Clint a beer.

"Yeah, thanks," Clint said.

Nobody seemed to be looking at him, so he turned and leaned his elbows on the bar. In the mirror he saw one man stand and approach the bar. He was a thin man in his forties, looked as if he had been in the same clothes for days.

"I could use a drink," the man said.

"That right?"

"I might be able to help ya," the man said, "but talkin' is thirsty business."

"What's your name?"

"Owen."

"Bartender," Clint said, "give Owen whatever he wants."

"All he ever wants is whiskey," the bartender said.

"Then give him one."

The bartender shrugged and poured a shot.

"Thanks," Owen said.

Clint stopped him as he brought the glass to his mouth.

"What've you got for me?"

"You're lookin' for two men?"

"That's right."

"They got names?"

"Ben Vincent and the Utah Kid."

"Yeah, that one," Owen said. "The Utah Kid. Fancies himself a fast gun."

"That's what I hear."

"You mind?" Owen asked, looking at the glass.

"Go ahead."

Owen downed the shot.

"Give him another one," Clint told the bartender.

The barman poured a second shot.

"Go ahead, Owen," Clint said, "Drink it."

Owen downed the second shot.

"Where do I find the Utah Kid and his friend?" Clint asked.

"They usually come in here after they finish at the whorehouse," Owen said.

"Where's the whorehouse?" Clint asked.

"You're probably better off waitin' for them right here," Owen said. "How about another drink?"

"One more," Clint said, "and then, after I have my men, you get a whole bottle."

Owen smiled and drank the third shot.

***

Clint sat at a table with Owen and got the man a beer to nurse while they waited. The saloon started to fill up.

"Do they have friends here?" Clint asked. "The Kid and his partner?"

"They stay to themselves," Owen said. "And people avoid them."

"How often do they come to this town?"

"They come and go," Owen said. "Sometimes a short time, sometimes longer."

"Do they have any dealings with the sheriff?"

Owen laughed.

"The sheriff hardly ever comes out of his office, except to eat."

"I see."

Owen sipped his now lukewarm beer.

"I'll get us each another cold one," Clint said, standing.

"You might wanna wait on that beer," Owen said, "and get ready to buy me a bottle."

Clint sat and looked toward the door. Two men had just entered, one in his thirties and the other probably twenty or so.

"The Utah Kid?" Clint asked.

"He really is a kid," Owen said, "but he's dangerous."

As the two outlaws walked toward the bar, several men stepped out of their way, quickly.

"That's a lot of fear," Clint said.

"Yeah," Owen said, "of the kid, not the other fella."

"Has the Kid killed anyone in town?"

"Probably," Owen said.

"Probably?"

"Well, I know he gunned down at least one man, but that was face-to-face in the streets. There have been some others who turned up dead after crossing him, but no proof he did it."

"And if there was proof the sheriff wouldn't act on it."

"No."

"Okay," Clint said, "I'll get you your bottle, and then you leave."

"Right."

Clint stood up and walked to the far end of the bar.

"A bottle," he said to the bartender.

"Right."

The bartender brought him a bottle and Clint grabbed his arm.

"Not a word," he said.

"I told you," the man said. "I don't know nothin'. You got my word."

"Keep it that way."

Clint walked back to the table and handed Owen the bottle.

"Go!" he said.

Chapter Thirty-One

Clint waited until Owen had left the saloon with his bottle, then turned his attention to his two prey. He could have gotten the drop on the men, but from everything he had heard about the Utah Kid, he wouldn't have given in so easily.

He continued to observe as the two men settled in at the bar, leaning comfortably over their beers.

Clint could read the Utah Kid's body language very clearly. He had the chin and shoulders of a man who thought he was untouchable. On the other hand, the older man seemed content to remain inside himself. He wondered why Ben Vincent chose to keep company with the Kid in between their Six jobs?

Studying the contrast between the two men, Clint decided he would be better off approaching Ben Vincent away from the Utah Kid. The question was, when would that be? Did the men stay together from morning to night? Or did they split up at some point? The only way to determine that was to keep watching them until such time as they parted ways. It was certainly possible that they each had their own room, somewhere.

While keeping an eye on the two men, Clint also watched the bartender. The barman exchanged very few words with the men, so Clint assumed he was keeping his word.

***

It took until midnight for something to happen.

The older Vincent turned and said something to the Utah Kid. The Kid nodded, and then Vincent left the saloon with Clint on his tail.

There were two hotels in town, Clint had a room in one, and Ben Vincent headed for the other one.

As Vincent entered the lobby, Clint remained outside, giving the man a chance to get settled. Eventually, he entered and approached the desk.

"Help you, Sir?" the young clerk asked.

"The man who just came in," Clint said. "What room is he in?"

"That would be Mr. Vincent, Sir," the clerk replied. "I'm really not supposed to say—"

"Don't worry about it," Clint said, cutting him off and taking a dollar from his pocket. "Just tell me his room number."

The man hesitated, then took the dollar and said, "Room five, Sir."

"Thanks."

Clint went up the stairs, walked to room five and knocked on the door.

"What the hell—" Ben Vincent was saying, as he opened the door, but he stopped short when he saw Clint standing in the hall. He seemed to suddenly become aware that his gunbelt was on the bed. "Who're you? Whataya want?"

"I want you to back up and let me in. Don't even think about your gun."

"You're makin' a big mistake," Vincent said, as he stepped back.

"Just move over to one side," Clint said, closing the door. He quickly snatched the man's gunbelt up from the bed.

"Whataya want?" Vincent asked, again.

"You and your partner," Clint said. "I already got Kingman, Reese and Patch. You and the Kid will make five, and then I'm going after Rome."

Rather than deny anything, Vincent said, "You'll never get to Rome because you won't get past the Kid."

"We'll see."

"I'm tellin' ya," Vincent said, "he's fast."

"So I've heard."

"Who the hell are ya?" Vincent asked. "A bounty hunter?"

"Everybody asks me that," Clint said. "I'm not a bounty hunter or a lawman, just a law-abiding citizen."

Vincent frowned.

"What's your name?"

"Clint Adams."

That surprised Vincent.

"The Kid is gonna love this," he said. "You'll have to get the drop on him, though, or he'll kill ya. I mean, he's a lot younger than you, and probably faster."

"That remains to be seen," Clint commented. "Sit on the bed."

"Why? So I don't have far to fall when you kill me?"

"I want you comfortable, so you can tell me where to find Harry Rome."

Vincent sat on the bed.

"I don't know where Rome is," he said. "It's him who knows where we are."

"Are you sure?" Clint asked. "He's never said anything about where he stays between jobs?"

"Not a clue," Vincent said. "You'll have to kill me and then face the Kid."

"I'm putting you in a cell," Clint said. "I don't have to kill you."

"And the others? What do you mean, you got 'em?"

"Patch and Reese are behind bars."

"And Kingman?"

"I don't know if he survived," Clint said. "I shot him, but he was still alive when I left him."

"So now that you have me, there's only the Kid and Rome." Vincent smiled. "One of them will kill you."

"Like I said," Clint replied, "we'll see."

Chapter Thirty-Two

Clint tied Ben Vincent hand and foot and then laid him on the bed.

"Now what?" Vincent asked.

"Now I'll go and see this Utah Kid," Clint said. "Is that really his name?"

"It's the only one he lays claim to."

"And you don't know his real name?"

"No idea."

"Does Rome know?"

"Probably."

"Then maybe the Kid knows where I can find Rome."

"He'd never tell you."

"That's for me to find out."

Vincent started to say something else, but Clint cut him off by gagging him.

"Just relax," he told Vincent. "I'll be back here with the Kid, and then we'll talk some more."

Mmmm-mmmph," Vincent mumbled.

"Answer my questions with a nod or shake of your head," Clint said.

Vincent stared.

"You said the Kid is fast."

Vincent nodded.

"Is he smart?"

A slight hesitation, and then a shake of his head.

"So without you to guide him, he'll make the wrong decision."

Vincent nodded.

"All right," Clint said, "I'll be back."

***

Clint made his way to the Cactus Saloon, hoping to find the Kid still there. As he entered, he saw the young man still standing at the bar. There was no time like the present.

"Utah Kid!" he shouted.

It got quiet in the now crowded saloon. The Kid froze, a beer mug halfway to his mouth, and then turned to see who had called his name.

"That's what they call you, isn't it?" Clint asked.

"It's what I call myself," the Kid said. "What do you call yourself?"

"My name's Clint Adams. I don't call myself anything else."

"They call you the Gunsmith," the Kid said.

"That may be," Clint said, "but I have a name. Have you? Other than being one of The Six, do you have a name?"

"I'm the Utah Kid," the Kid said. "That's all you need to know. And after today," he smiled, "I'll be the man who killed the Gunsmith."

"You only need to tell me where to find Harry Rome," Clint said, "and I won't kill you. You might live to be twenty-one."

The Kid laughed. The saloon patrons abandoned their tables and pressed themselves against the walls.

"Aren't you wondering at all where Ben Vincent is?" Clint asked.

"I assume you killed him, already."

"He's alive," Clint said. "I'm turning him over to the law. I'll do the same for you, if you give up."

The Utah Kid laughed.

"You're twice my age," he said, "and half as fast. Let's show these folks how right I am."

"Where's Rome, Kid?"

"I don't know that," the Kid said. "Rome knows where we are and contacts us when he wants us. All you need to do is kill me, and then wait to hear from him."

"I see."

"But you can't kill me," the Kid said. "I'm the fastest gun alive."

Clint knew they had gone far enough.

"Show me," he said.

***

Harry Rome cut into his steak, popped a bloody chunk into his mouth and chewed thoughtfully. He had two possible jobs in mind for The Six. All he had to do was decide which one to pick, and then contact the others to meet him.

"More potatoes, Mr. Rome?" the waiter asked.

Rome sat back, looked up at the waiter.

"That'd be great."

The waiter spooned half a dozen boiled potatoes onto Rome's plate.

"I'll bring more coffee," the man said.

"Please."

As the waiter walked away, Rome turned his attention to the new potatoes on his plate.

He had a bank in mind, and a payroll that was going to be delivered by stage. If he went for the payroll, he would need the men to gather in a week. If he couldn't get them together, he would have to go for the bank.

But first he would have to finish his meal before he sent the telegrams out.

Chapter Thirty-Three

Clint was impressed with the Kid's move. He was so fast that Clint had no choice but to kill him.

The shots were almost simultaneous, but when they faded, the Kid was face down on the floor, Clint was standing over him, gun in hand. The place was quiet, and then there was the sound of shuffling feet as the patrons moved closer for a look.

"Jesus Christ!" somebody breathed.

"That was *fast*!" someone else whispered.

"He was fast," Clint said, ejecting his spent shell, "but he was also a fool." He reloaded and holstered his gun. "You all saw it. If the sheriff asks. It was a fair fight."

"The sheriff ain't gonna say a thin'," the bartender said.

"A few of you men pick him up and take him to the undertaker. The rest of you go back to your drinkin'."

Clint stepped to the bar.

"Beer?" the bartender asked.

"With a whiskey," Clint said.

The bartender set both glasses down on the bar.

"That was somethin' to see," he said to Clint.

"Maybe," Clint said, "but nothing to be proud of. That boy could have had a long life ahead of him."

"Not with his attitude," the bartender said. "He was lookin' to die."

Clint drank the whiskey and then a sip of beer.

"Whataya gonna do now?" the barman asked.

"I've got his partner tied up at the hotel," Clint said. "I'll turn him over to the law."

The bartender laughed.

"Our sheriff?" he asked.

"Federal law," Clint said. "Then I've got one more to find."

"You've been huntin' The Six?"

"That's right."

"For a bounty?"

"A favor for two governors," Clint said. "What do I owe you for the drinks?"

"On the house," the bartender said. "I'll be tellin' this story for years."

"Thanks," Clint said, and left the Cactus.

***

When Clint entered the room, Ben Vincent turned his head and stared. Clint removed his gag.

"I heard shots," Vincent said.

"Yes, you did."

"The Kid?"

"Dead," Clint said, "because he was a fool."

Vincent looked disappointed.

"So now you'll kill me, unless I can give you Rome?" he asked.

"I'm not going to kill you," Clint said. "I'm turning you over to the law to stand trial. You, Patch, Reese and Kingman, if he's still alive."

"And then?"

"And then I'll find Harry Rome, whether you help me or not."

"Harry ain't as fast as the Kid was," Vincent said. "But he's smart."

"If he's that smart," Clint asked, "why didn't he pick five smarter men?"

"Smart men think they're smarter than anyone," Vincent said. "He needed five men who would just be smart enough to do what they're told."

"And now that he doesn't have those men?"

"He'll just find five more," Vincent said.

Clint took a wooden chair from the corner, placed it next to the bed and sat.

"How long has it been since your last job?" he asked.

"A month, maybe more."

"How long does he usually wait between jobs?"

"It depends on how big the last one was," Vincent said, "and how big the next one will be."

"Weeks? Months?"

"He's never waited more than a couple of months," Vincent said.

"So, he's likely to send a message here for you and the Kid in, say, a month?"

"That's likely."

Clint sat back and crossed a leg.

"So, if I just wait here for a month," he said, "I'll know where he is."

"You'll know where he wants us to meet him," Vincent answered.

"A month," Clint said, thoughtfully. "I don't know if I have that much patience."

"It'd probably be worth your while to find out," Vincent said.

After a moment's thought Clint asked, "Are you hungry?"

"Starved."

Clint stood.

"I killed your friend," he said. "Will you try to kill me?"

"He wasn't my friend," Vincent said. "Rome told me to travel with him and keep him alive."

"So he won't be happy to hear you failed."

"No," Vincent said, "he won't."

Clint rolled Vincent over and untied him.

"Let's get a steak," he said.

Chapter Thirty-Four

When they finished their steaks, they both sat back in their chairs.

"Why are you feedin' me?" Vincent asked.

"Because you're a smart man, smart enough to want to keep eating."

"They'll feed me in prison."

"But not this well."

"No."

The waiter came over.

"Anythin' else, gents?"

"Two slices of pie," Clint said, "and more coffee."

"What kind of pie, sir?"

"Whatever your cook does best," Clint said, "as long as it's not rhubarb."

"Yes, Sir."

"I hate rhubarb," Vincent said.

"So do I."

"I've told you the truth, you know," Vincent said. "I don't know where to find Harry Rome."

"I believe you," Clint said.

"Then why treat me so well?" Vincent asked.

"You might do me more good this way than if you're in a cell," Clint said.

"You want me to turn on Harry Rome?"

"I want you to make a decision," Clint said. "Help me or go right to prison. Maybe even hang for the murders The Six committed."

"Harry did the killin'," Vincent said, "along with Bax Kingman and the Kid. Me, Patch and Reese watched the door, and the horses, and kept men at bay."

"You never killed anyone?"

Vincent hesitated, then said, "Not as one of the Six."

The waiter appeared with two loaded slices of apple pie, and coffee.

"Eat your pie," Clint said. "Then I'll take you back to your room."

"And tie me up?"

"Not if you give me your word you won't try to escape."

"What if I do try?"

Clint shrugged.

"Then I'd have no choice but to kill you."

Vincent chewed his pie.

"You have my word."

"Good."

"I promised Rome to look after the Kid," Vincent said, "I suppose I'm not bound by that promise, anymore."

***

The nearest town to Big Bend that had a telegraph line was Gallup. When Clint rode there, he took Ben Vincent with him. The man never made a move to escape.

Clint sent a telegram to the Texas capital, describing his accomplishments and explaining his plan. Vincent was still waiting outside when he left the telegraph office.

"Are we waitin' for a reply?" he asked.

"We are," Clint said. "I think a meal and a beer will do it."

"You feed me well."

"And I'll continue to do so as long as you cooperate," Clint said.

"I will," Vincent promised.

Clint allowed the man to wear his gun, as a show of good faith.

"The telegraph operator said there's a good café down the street," Clint said. "We'll wait there for the reply, then head back to Big Bend."

"What if it doesn't come today?" Vincent asked.

"It'll come."

"Then let's eat."

***

They had finished their meal and were washing it down with coffee when the telegraph operator appeared in the doorway. He spotted Clint and walked across the floor to him.

"Your response from the capital, Sir," he said, holding it out.

Clint accepted it and paid the man.

"Thank you."

As the operator left, Clint read the reply.

"So?" Vincent asked.

"They're a little impatient about how much longer it may take," Clint said, folding the telegram, "but they're also pleased that I've managed to catch five."

"Do they know about me?" Vincent asked.

"They know I've caught five of The Six," Clint said. "That's all."

"And what will they say when they do find out about me?" Vincent asked.

"By then I'll have Harry Rome," Clint said. "They won't care much about you."

Chapter Thirty-Five

They were back in Big Bend a week when a rider came in looking for Ben Vincent. Clint and Vincent had taken to whiling away the time playing two-handed poker in the Cactus Saloon.

The rider stopped at the bar, had a beer, then spoke with the bartender, who pointed to the table where Clint and Vincent were sitting. The man finished his beer and walked over to the table.

"Ben Vincent?" he asked.

"That's me," Vincent said.

"I got a message for you or the Utah Kid," the man said. "But I heard the Kid was dead."

"He is."

"Guess this is yours."

He handed Vincent a telegram, then turned and left.

"What's it say?" Clint asked.

Vincent handed it to Clint without reading it.

"He wants you in a town called Harrandale, Texas in one week's time."

"Where the hell is that?" Vincent asked.

"We'll find out," Clint said. "Maybe there's a bank there."

"He never meets us in the town where we're gonna pull the job," Vincent said. "Always one nearby."

"Then we'll find Harrandale," Clint said, "and Harry Rome. It won't matter what job he's planning next."

***

Harrandale turned out to be at least a week's ride from Big Bend. Ben Vincent had a dun who looked like he could make the trip alongside Clint's Tobiano.

"That's a pretty young animal," Vincent said, as they saddled them.

"He'll get older," Clint said.

"Won't we all," Vincent said.

By the time they rode out of Big Bend, Clint was fairly sure he could count on Ben Vincent. Once he was no longer charged with looking after the Utah Kid, Vincent didn't seem all that loyal to Harry Rome.

In fact, during the ride, each night they camped, they got to know each other better.

"I have to say," Clint said on the fourth night, "you don't strike me as the type of man who would join The Six."

"I had nothin'," Vincent said. "Rome promised me money. All I had to do was look after the Kid."

"Why was the Kid important to Rome?"

"The Kid and Kingman would kill wherever Rome pointed," Vincent said. "That was important to him."

"The killing?"

"The killing or having somebody killed," Vincent said. "What about you?"

"What about me?" Clint said.

"You kill," Vincent said. "That is, accordin' to your reputation."

"Yes," Clint said. "But I always do my own killing, when it needs to be done."

"But you don't enjoy it."

"Not at all," Clint said.

"Never?"

Clint shook his head.

"Never," Clint said. "Like with the Utah Kid, I do it when I have no other choice."

"You could have disarmed him," Vincent said, "or wounded him."

"I couldn't do that," Clint said.

"Why not?"

"He was too quick to take chances with."

***

Harrandale was a fair-sized town, with several hotels and saloons. But there was no telegraph office.

As they rode past the sheriff's office Vincent asked, "Will we be stoppin' there?"

"Maybe later," Clint said. "Let's see if Harry Rome is here."

"He'd be in one of the saloons," Vincent said.

"Then let's try one."

They stopped at the first saloon they came to, the Red Arrow, and tied their horses outside. As they entered, people turned their heads to look, then turned back to their drinks or games.

"Well?" Clint said.

"He's not here."

"Let's get a beer before we move on."

They stepped up to the bar.

"Two beers," Clint said.

"Yes, Sir."

When they had their beers, they turned and studied the inside of the saloon.

"Is this his kind of place?" Clint asked.

"Looks like it."

"We'll check the other saloon. If he's not there, we'll come back here and wait."

"Okay by me."

"What will he do when he sees me sitting here with you?" Clint asked.

"He'll probably want to know who you are, and where the others are. If I was you, I'd gun him down as soon as I saw him."

"My intention is to bring him in."

"He'll never go," Vincent said.

"We'll see."

Chapter Thirty-Six

The second saloon, the Black Horse, was smaller and there was no sign of Rome. Of course, that was according to Ben Vincent. Clint didn't know what Harry Rome looked like. He'd have to take Vincent's word for it.

He was going to have to decide if he could trust Ben Vincent much longer.

They saw to their horses and got a hotel room each. With all that done, they returned to the Red Arrow.

They sat staring into their beers.

"What if he doesn't come?" Vincent asked.

"Why wouldn't he come?"

"Maybe he's heard that you caught the others," Vincent said. "All of us."

"The word hasn't been sent out that five of The Six have been caught," Clint assured him.

"Rome has eyes all over, lookin' for jobs, and bein' alert for news."

"If he knew, why would he have sent that telegram to you?" Clint asked. "No, he hasn't heard."

"When he walks in here, he'll see me," Vincent said, "and wonder who you are."

"So tell him."

"And?"

"And then we'll see," Clint said. "Maybe he'll think you're offering me up as a new member of The Six."

Vincent laughed.

"If he thought the Gunsmith was available, he'd snatch you up," he said. "Is there any reason to foster that lie?"

"No," Clint said. "He's the only one left."

"And me," Vincent reminded him.

"We'll see about you," Clint said.

They got to the end of the night without Harry Rome appearing.

"He might be watching, waiting for all five to arrive," Vincent said. "Or he might be wondering who you are."

"If he is, let him ask," Clint said. He finished his last beer. "I'm going to turn in."

"I think I'll have another beer," Vincent said.

"Suit yourself," Clint said, standing. "I better see you in the morning."

"I'll be at the hotel, Clint."

Clint left the saloon, crossed the street and chose a darkened doorway. He intended to watch and see if Ben Vincent met Harry Rome that night, after he supposedly turned in. This would confirm which side Ben Vincent was on.

***

Clint woke the next morning no more assured of Ben Vincent than before. The man had consumed a few more beers the night before, and then turned in, unaware Clint was watching.

He found Vincent waiting for him the next morning in the lobby.

"I thought we'd get breakfast together," the man said.

"Suits me."

"We might run into Rome."

"That'd suit me, too," Clint said.

They left the hotel and walked til they came to a café.

"Looks good enough," he said.

Vincent nodded, and they entered. Many townspeople were occupying tables. They found one in the back.

"Ham-and-eggs," Clint told the waiter.

"The same," Vincent said.

"And coffee," Clint added, "hot and strong."

"Yes, Sir.

The waiter went off to fill their orders.

"Did you stay in the saloon late last night?" Clint asked.

"I did," Vincent said. "Harry never showed."

"Maybe he will today."

"Harry's a smart man, Clint," Vincent said. "You better watch him carefully."

"I intend to."

"You'd be smart to kill 'im on sight."

"You may be right," Clint said, "but the governors want him in jail for his crimes."

"They'll hang him, anyway," Vincent said. "What's the difference?"

"The trial," Clint said. "The trial is the difference."

The waiter came with the coffee. They waited while he poured and went back to the kitchen.

"I'll probably go on trial, too," Vincent said.

"Probably," Clint said, "but I'll speak for you the more you help me."

"Let's hope your word carries some weight," Ben Vincent said.

The waiter returned with their plates, and a basket of warm biscuits.

"Enjoy your breakfast, gents," the waiter said, and walked away.

Clint and Vincent put their attention toward their breakfast.

Chapter Thirty-Seven

After breakfast Clint and Vincent checked with the desk clerk at their hotel as to whether or not there was a whorehouse in town.

"No whorehouse," the clerk said, "just a couple of whores who have their own huts on the north side of town."

"Okay, thanks," Clint said, and they stepped outside. "What do you think?"

"Harry Rome bedding a dirty street whore?" Vincent said. "Not likely."

"So," Clint said, "we continue to wait in one of the saloons?"

Vincent shrugged.

"That'd be my best bet," the man said.

Clint looked up and down the busy main street of Harrandale.

"It's a quiet town," he said, looking across the street. "And it has a bank."

"I told you," Vincent said. "Harry never meets us in the same town where he plans to pull a job. So don't even think about this bank."

"It's a little early to hit the saloons," Clint said. He looked up and down the street again. "I wonder what's keeping Rome?"

***

Harry Rome rolled over and looked at the woman lying next to him. He was in a hotel room in the town of Merrindale, Texas. It was considered the sister town of Harrandale, which was five miles away.

The woman was a saloon girl he met the night before in the Saddlebag Saloon. She was long and lean and, for the right amount of money, was willing to go to his hotel with him. He fucked her until she screamed, and then they fell asleep. Now he lay awake while she continued to snore gently.

Rome was feeling uneasy. What no one knew was that when he contacted his five cohorts, Bax Kingman would always send a reply. This time that response had not come. That could only mean one thing: Kingman was dead or in jail. It remained to be seen if Patch, Reese, the Utah Kid and Ben Vincent were in Harrandale waiting for him. Kingman could have gotten himself killed or arrested as a result of a bar fight. But Rome felt there was more than that at play. The Six had been successful for many months, no matter who had been sent after them. But that kind of success could not last forever. He didn't know what he would be riding into when he left for Harrandale. That was why he had stopped here, first.

"Are you watchin' me sleep?" the girl asked, without turning her head.

"Yes," he lied, "I am."

Now she turned and looked at him. She was a pretty girl in her thirties who had, for many years, been a saloon girl/whore. She was very good at both jobs.

She reached out to run her hand down over his chest and belly, until she had her fingers wrapped around his cock.

"Are you leavin' today?" she asked.

"I'm not sure."

She stroked him and said, "Maybe I can help you make up your mind."

"Let's see," he said, putting his hands behind his head.

She smiled and rolled over. She had small, dark-tipped breasts. As she slid over him, her hard nipples scraped his thighs. Once she was settled down between his outstretched legs she opened her mouth, sucked the bulbous head of his penis until it gleamed with her spit, then took the length of him into her mouth. Rome gave himself up to her expert ministrations, setting aside for the moment his thoughts of The Six. As she brought him to the brink of exploding, he realized he didn't remember her name. But as he reached down for her head and erupted into her mouth, he simply roared loudly . . .

***

"Annie," he said, moments later as it came to him.

"What?" she asked, while lying on her back.

"I just wanted to say your name," he told her.

She rolled onto her side.

"Have I convinced you to stay longer?"

"I have some business in Harrandale," he said.

"What kind of business?"

"I have to meet a man," he said, "but I'm wonderin' if it's safe."

"I knew it," she said.

"What?"

"You're either a lawman or on the run."

"Does it matter to you which?"

"Not at all," she said, stroking his thigh. "Maybe I can help."

"How?"

"Well," she said, "I could ride to Harrandale and check it out for you."

"And why would you do that?"

She dug her nails into his flesh.

"I'm tired of bein' a saloon girl and a whore," she said. "Maybe if I help you, you'll take me with you when you leave?"

He doubted that would ever happen, but he kind of liked the first part of her offer.

Chapter Thirty-Eight

Clint and Ben Vincent were sitting in chairs in front of the hotel when a woman rode in on a brown mare.

"You think this is smart?" Vincent asked, as the woman rode by. "Sittin' out in the open?"

"We can see everyone, and everyone can see us," Clint explained.

"So if Rome rides into town, you think he'll come right up to us?"

"When he sees you, maybe," Clint said.

"And then you'll take 'im?"

"We'll see."

Vincent looked down the street as the woman continued to the livery.

"That girl is the only one to ride into town since we got here yesterday," he complained.

Clint turned and watched as she dismounted and walked her horse into the livery stable.

"That's a good point, Ben." He looked at Vincent. "Would he choose to send a woman ahead as a scout?"

Ben Vincent's eyebrows went up.

"You know," he said, "that's somethin' he might very well do."

"Interesting," Clint said. "Since we don't have any other options, let's see if this one plays out."

They sat, watched and waited. Eventually the woman came out of the stable and started walking. She was tall and lean, clad in riding clothes and wearing a Stetson. She was not wearing a gunbelt nor carrying a rifle. Neither did she have any saddlebags.

"She travels light," Vincent said.

"Maybe she hasn't come very far."

She mounted the boardwalk and came toward them. Clint saw that she was a pretty woman in her thirties. When she reached them she stopped.

"How's this hotel?" she asked.

"I've stayed in better," Clint said.

She looked across the street.

"What about that one?"

"The same," Vincent said. "One's as good or bad as the other."

"Then I guess I'll stay in this one," she said, "since I'm already on this side of the street." She nodded to them. "Have a good day."

"And you," Clint replied.

She entered the hotel lobby.

"Whataya think?" Vincent asked.

"Pretty girl," Clint said. "That's all I can say now. Let's just keep an eye on her."

"Agreed."

***

Annie Stark entered the hotel and went to the front desk.

"Can I help you, Ma'am?" the clerk asked.

"I'm lookin' for a man," she said.

"Any man in particular?" the middle-aged clerk asked.

She hesitated and then said, "My husband."

"Ah . . . is he running from you?"

"Just as fast as he can," she said. "When I catch him, I'm gonna cut off his manhood."

"I hope you find him."

"I'm starting here," she said. "May I look at the register?"

"Sure," he said. "Why not?"

He turned the book so she could open it and read it. She ran her finger down the page and found what she was looking for . . . and more.

***

When they heard the horse, they looked up, saw the woman riding from the livery back up the street past them at a gallop.

"Looks like she went out the back door of the hotel and back to the stable," Clint said.

"Should we mount up and follow?"

"No." Clint stood and went into the lobby. Ben Vincent stayed where he was.

"Did the woman who came in here ask any questions?" he asked the clerk.

"She looked at the register," the man replied. "She said she was looking for her husband."

"And then she went out the back door?"

"Yes."

Clint nodded, returned to where Ben Vincent was still sitting.

"She's on her way to tell Rome you're here," he said.

"And you?"

"I'm sure she recognized my name," Clint said.

"So Harry'll know we're both here."

"What will he do then?"

"He'll come," Vincent said, "but he won't come alone."

Chapter Thirty-Nine

"Clint Adams?"

"That was the name I saw on the register," Annie said to Rome, "right below Ben Vincent."

"Did you see either of them?"

"I talked to two men who were sitting in front of the hotel. I don't know if that was them."

"Describe 'em to me."

She did.

"That was Ben," he said. "The other man must've been the Gunsmith."

"Is he looking for you?" she asked.

"I assume he is."

They were seated at a table in the Saddlebag Saloon. She had not taken the time to change her clothes. Rome found her more attractive this way than in her saloon girl dress.

"So what will you do? Run?"

"Yes," Rome said, "I'll run right to Harrandale."

"And face the Gunsmith alone?"

"No," he said, "not alone."

"Then with who?"

"I have an idea," he said.

"I can shoot," she told him.

He reached out and took her hand.

"You've done enough," he said. "I won't expect you to shoot, but I might have another job for you."

"What's that?"

He squeezed her hand.

"I'll let you know."

***

Later that day he came into the saloon again and pulled Annie over to the side. She was still in her riding clothes. He handed her a slip of paper.

"I want you to deliver this," he said.

"Where?"

"A town ten miles from here," he said. "It's called Winterville. There's a man there called Rankin. He'll read this and then ride back here with you."

"Are you sure?"

"You both should be back here by dark. But you have to leave now!"

She took the note from him, put it in her pocket, and ran from the saloon.

***

Rome was sitting in the empty saloon at two a.m. when the batwing doors swung inward, admitting Annie and a large, dark-haired man.

"Rome," the man said.

"Rankin," Rome replied.

"Is this true?" Rankin asked, dropping the note on the table. "The Gunsmith's in Harrandale?"

"Yes, he is."

Rankin smiled, causing his face to look wolflike.

"The others will be here later," he said. "Will he still be in Harrandale?"

"He'll be there until I get there," Rome said.

"Then let's have a drink."

Rankin sat and Annie went to the bar for a bottle.

"What's this about?" Rankin asked.

"The Six," Rome said.

Rankin looked surprised.

"That's you?"

"It was," Rome said. "It'll be again, if you'll join."

"But first we have to deal with the Gunsmith."

"Right."

Annie came over with the bottle and three glasses.

"What about her?" Rankin asked.

"She'll be around."

That seemed to satisfy Annie.

***

In the Red Arrow Saloon Clint asked Ben Vincent, "If he won't come alone, how long will it take him to collect some guns?"

"Not long," Vincent said. "He usually has some guns available. All it takes is a message."

"So there's more than six in The Six?" Clint asked.

"No," Vincent said, "they're not part of the Six. They're just guns for hire."

"Anybody I know?"

"Maybe," Vincent said. "You heard of Lou Rankin?"

"Rankin," Clint said, nodding, "I know the name."

"I always kept the Kid in check around Rankin," Vincent said, "I didn't wanna find out who was faster."

"You never will, now," Clint said.

"Sure I will."

"How?"

"If Rankin kills you," Vincent said, "he's the fastest."

Chapter Forty

After the saloon Clint went back to the hotel with Ben Vincent and spoke with the clerk about changing rooms.

"I never take a room overlooking the street," he told Vincent, "but tonight I want one."

"You think Rome's gonna sneak in after dark?" Vincent asked.

"I just want to be ready," Clint said. "How many men do you think he'll bring with him?"

"That's hard to say," Vincent said, "but we do know he likes the number six, right?"

"Apparently."

"He may ride in with six," Vincent said, "but he'll be leadin' the way."

"Good."

"But he won't sneak in at night," Vincent said. "You better get some sleep."

"I will," Clint said. "After I keep watch for a short time."

"Good-night, then," Vincent said. "I'll see you in the mornin'."

They went their separate ways, Vincent to his room, and Clint to his new one.

For a few hours he sat at the window looking down at the street. Finally, he decided Ben Vincent was right. Harry Rome would not sneak into Harrandale. He would ride right down the main street.

He turned and went to bed.

***

Rome looked up from his breakfast table. Annie saw the look in his eyes and followed his gaze. Rankin was walking across the café floor to them.

"Are they here?" Rome asked.

"They're here."

"Sit, then," Rome said. "Have some breakfast before we go."

"Just like that?" Rankin asked. "Just ride into town in broad daylight?"

"Yup," Rome said. "Just like that."

The waiter came over, and Rankin pointed to Rome's plate of flapjacks.

"The same."

"Yessir."

Rankin looked at Annie, whose eyes were on her plate of bacon-and-eggs.

"I'm gonna have to explain to the men what her part is," he said to Rome.

"She's with me," Rome said. "That's all they need to know."

The waiter came and set the plate in front of Rankin. The man started to eat.

***

Rome and Annie followed Rankin into the livery where five men were saddling their fresh mounts. They stopped and turned.

"This is Harry Rome," Rankin said. "He's the one payin' us." He stepped aside.

"The Gunsmith is in Harrandale with one of my men," he said. "He's waiting for me to show up."

"And when we do?" one asked.

"We'll see what happens," Rome said. "None of you draw a gun until I do. Understood?"

They all nodded.

"Who's gonna take the Gunsmith, you or Rankin?" another asked.

"Like I said," Rome said, "it all remains to be seen."

"Why is the Gunsmith looking for you?" a third asked.

"You don't need to know that," Rome said.

He noticed a few of the men looking at Annie.

"You all get paid if you do what you're told, when you're told," Rome said.

Rankin glared at them all. They didn't know Harry Rome, but they knew Rankin, and were afraid of him.

"Everybody understand?" Rankin asked.

They jerked their eyes away from Annie and nodded their heads.

"Good," Rome said. "Walk your mounts outside and wait for us."

The five men walked their horses out of the stable.

"Should I saddle the lady's horse?" Rankin asked.

"I can saddle my own horse," Annie insisted.

"Whatever you say," Rankin replied.

The three of them saddled their horses and prepared to walk them out.

"Are they good with their guns?" Rome asked.

"They can all shoot," Rankin said. "But good?" He shrugged. "But they'll do what you tell them to do."

"As long as I have you standin' next to me," Rome said.

"As long as you pay them."

"They'll get paid," Rome said.

They walked their horses outside, where they all mounted up and rode out of Merrindale.

Chapter Forty-One

Clint woke and walked to the window. It was early and the town was just coming awake. He dressed then went to meet Ben Vincent in the lobby.

When he got to the lobby Vincent wasn't there.

"Has Mr. Vincent come down from his room?" he asked the clerk.

"Not that I know of, Sir."

Clint went back upstairs and knocked on Vincent's door. When there was no answer, he tried the knob and found the door unlocked. He entered the room, it was empty, the bed not slept in. Vincent's gear was not there.

Clint wondered if Vincent had left town, or gone to meet Harry Rome? Could he afford to let the man go when the governors had tasked him with catching The Six—all six of them?

He left the room and went back downstairs. He decided to have breakfast, so as to face Harry Rome on a full stomach.

He went to the café where he and Vincent had eaten before. The man wasn't there, so he took a back table and ordered.

He ate slowly, watching others come and go. When he finished, he paid his bill and stepped outside. As he did, he saw the riders coming down the street. There were seven men and the girl he and Vincent had spoken to in front of the hotel. Two men rode in front. He was sure one of them was Harry Rome.

At the same time, he saw a man approaching him on foot, wearing a badge.

"Clint Adams?"

"That's right."

He was a tall man, maybe six-and-a-half feet tall, had the look of an experienced lawman.

"Sheriff Snow," the man said. "I just got back after a week away and heard you were in town. Can we talk?"

Clint watched the column of men ride by, following Harry Rome, who was staring back.

"Is there a problem?" Snow asked.

"Not at all."

"Then will you come to my office with me?"

Clint said, "Lead the way, Sheriff."

"This way . . ."

***

As they entered the sheriff's office Clint realized it had been locked while the lawman was away.

"No deputies?" Clint asked.

"Not in a town this size."

The man sat behind his desk, cleaned the dust off it with a sweep of a long-sleeved arm.

"If I had been here when you arrived, I would've asked you something," Sheriff Snow said.

"Go ahead and ask."

"What's the Gunsmith doin' in Harrandale?"

"Lookin' for someone."

"The someone who just rode in?"

"You saw him?"

The man smiled.

"Kind of hard not to," he said. "Who is he?"

"His name's Harry Rome."

"I don't know him."

"He's the leader of a group called The Six," Clint explained.

"Ah," Snow said, "and where are the other five?"

"In jail, or dead," Clint said. "Rome is the last."

"And why have you been after The Six?"

Clint showed the lawman his letter signed by the governors."

"Impressive," Snow said, handing it back. "I notice the letter doesn't say dead or alive."

"That's up to them," Clint said. "So far it's been alive."

"He has six men with him," the sheriff said, "and a woman, I noticed. Do you think you can take him alive?"

"As I said," Clint replied, "that'll be up to him."

"Do you have anyone backin' your play?"

Clint thought about Ben Vincent.

"No," Clint said, "but I won't need anyone."

"That's good," the lawman said, "because I won't stand on either side. I'll just arrest the winner."

"For what?"

"I'll come up with somethin'," the sheriff said. But try to do us all a favor."

"What's that?"

"Settle your differences without bullets."

"I seem to be saying this to everyone," Clint said, turning to the door, "but that'll be up to him.

***

As Rome and his party unsaddled their horses at the livery, Rankin said, "You saw the sheriff?"

"I did."

"And was that Adams he was talkin' to?"

"I don't know, but that would be my bet." He looked at Annie.

"He was one of the men I talked to when I was here," she said.

"One of the men you spoke to was Ben Vincent," Rome said, "so I assume the other was Adams."

"He might have the law on his side," Rankin said.

"Does that bother you?" Rome asked.

"Not a bit."

They left the livery together, stood outside.

"Are we gonna take 'im right away?" one of the men asked.

"I'm going to talk to him first," Rome said. "You five go and get a drink, and some rooms for yourselves."

"And a room for the lady?" one asked, smiling at Annie.

"She'll be with me, and Rankin," Rome said. "Don't worry about her."

"And don't get into any trouble," Rankin told them.

"Right," one of them said, and the others nodded.

The five men headed for the town. Rome, Rankin and Annie walked behind them, more slowly.

"Are you really gonna talk to him first?" she asked.

"Yes."

"Why not have Rankin kill him from behind while you do that?"

"You don't kill the Gunsmith from behind," Rankin said. "You do it face-to-face, man-to-man."

"That sounds stupid," Annie said.

"That's one of the reasons you're not a man," Rankin said.

She smiled at him and said, "Oh, there are more reasons than that."

Chapter Forty-Two

When Clint left the sheriff's office, he thought about what the man had asked him about having back-up. At one time he thought that Ben Vincent would back his play. But now that seemed unlikely. He was either going to have to stand alone against Harry Rome, or against Rome and his men. If the latter was the case, it would be seven against one.

He felt foolish for thinking he might have lured Ben Vincent over to his side. The man had either left town, or he was joining up with Harry Rome. It remained to be seen.

He wondered where Rome and his people had gone? A hotel? Saloon? One of those two seemed the most likely.

But of the eight people who had ridden into town, the only one who held his interest was Harry Rome.

He checked his hotel first, asking the clerk for a look at the register. Sure enough, Harry Rome's name was there. Beneath it was the name Rankin. There was no woman's name. She was probably sharing Rome's room. There also were not five other names there, so he assumed the other men were at the hotel across the street.

He considered going to Harry Rome's room and knocking on the door. Then he decided to leave it to Rome to find him. So he left the hotel and went to the Red Arrow. As he entered, he looked for the men who had ridden in with Rome. None were there. He went to the bar, got a beer and took it to a table, the one he usually shared with Ben Vincent.

***

Rome opened his door to Rankin's knock and let him in. Annie sat on the bed, fully dressed.

"What now?" Rankin asked.

"Now I have a talk with the Gunsmith," Rome said, "see if I can convince him of the folly of his actions."

"And if you can't?"

"Then I'll show it to him."

"When?" Rankin asked.

"Now's as good a time as any," Rome said, "He's probably finished with the sheriff."

Annie stood up.

"No," Rome said, "you stay here."

"I can shoot," Annie said.

"You have no gun."

"I can handle a rifle."

"I want you to stay here, and be safe," Rome said. "I'll be back."

"What if you're not?" she asked.

"Then Lou will take you back to Merrindale."

I don't want to go back there."

"He'll take you wherever you want to go," Rome said. "Just stay here." He looked at Rankin. "Let's go."

***

Clint was halfway through his beer when the batwing doors swung inward and Rome walked in, followed by another man. He looked around the mostly empty Red Arrow and walked over to Clint's table.

"Clint Adams?"

"That's right."

"My name's Harry Rome," the man said. "This is Lou Rankin."

Clint sat back.

"Glad to meet you," Clint said. "Have a seat, and a beer."

Clint waved at the bartender, who brought over three fresh beers.

Rome and Rankin sat.

"I understand you've been lookin' for me," Harry Rome said.

Chapter Forty-Three

"That's right."

"And if I heard right, you've already caught five of The Six."

"Four," Clint said.

"How's that?"

"Reese, Patch, the Utah Kid, and Bax Kingman."

"You say Bax like you knew him."

"I did," Clint said. "Not well, but I knew him."

"Is he dead?"

"I don't know," Clint said. "I shot him, but he was alive when I left."

"And the others?"

"Reese and Patch are in a cell," he said. "The Utah Kid is dead."

"You outdrew him?"

"I did."

"The Kid was fast," Rankin said.

Clint looked at him.

"Yes, he was."

"What about Ben Vincent?" Rome asked.

"What about him?"

"He was here with you, wasn't he?"

"Yesterday," Clint said, "but today I don't know where he is."

Rome laughed.

"Ben got away from you?"

"Looks like it," Clint said. "I thought he might've gone to you."

"I haven't seen him," Rome said. "Maybe I'll find him after . . ."

"After what?"

"After we're done."

"We'll be done when I take you in, Rome," Clint said.

"Why do you want me?" Rome asked.

"You're the leader of The Six," Clint said. "The Governors of Texas and New Mexico have tasked me with bringing you to justice."

Rome raised his eyebrows.

"Impressive," he said. "Are you quite sure I'm the man you want?"

"Very sure."

"So you intend to kill me?"

"I told you," Clint said. "I've been asked to bring you to justice."

"And what if I won't go quietly?"

"Well," Clint said, "then we'll have to see what happens, won't we?"

Rome looked at Rankin.

"I've heard of you," Clint said to the other man.

"I'm flattered," Rankin said.

"I've heard you're fast."

"Very fast," Rankin said. "And accurate. I've never missed."

"Now that's impressive," Clint said. He looked at Rome. "Will he be acting for you?"

"No, no," Rome said. "I do my own dirty work. He's just here to make sure everythin' is on the up-and-up."

"As you can see," Clint said, "I'm alone. You rode in with five other men and a woman."

"Just to be sure I had enough men to defend myself if the need arose. But you're alone, so I won't need them."

"Just him," Clint said, inclining his head toward Rankin.

"Perhaps," Rome said, "Who knows?"

They all drank their beers.

"So," Rome said, "when do we do this?"

"You can both take your guns off now and lay them on the table," Clint said, "And it's done."

"That's not gonna happen," Rome said. "What's next?"

"I'll have to take you in," Clint said. "You could both draw on me now, and you might kill me. I know I'd kill at least one of you."

Rome and Rankin set their empty beer mugs down.

"I think we'll probably see about that," Rome said, "tomorrow. Right now let's have another beer."

He waved at the bartender.

***

Annie looked through the front window of the saloon, saw Rome and Rankin sitting with the man she had spoken to in front of the hotel. She had a rifle in her hands and knew she could shoot the man through the window. But Rome didn't want her to do that.

She held the rifle ready, though, just in case the need arose to use it.

***

"What about Ben?" Rome asked. "Will you continue to search for him?"

"If it comes to that, yes," Clint said. "I've been sent to catch all six."

"Seems like you had him and lost him," Rankin said.

Clint looked at Rankin and said, "Yeah, it seems that way."

Chapter Forty-Four

After they finished their second beers together, Rome and Rankin stood.

"Tomorrow," Rome said. "In the daylight."

"I'll be there," Clint said.

Rome turned to leave, but Rankin stared at Clint.

"Something else?" Clint asked.

"No," Rankin said, "not right now."

He turned and followed Rome out of the saloon. Clint waved at the bartender for another beer.

***

When Rome left the saloon, he ran right into Annie Stark.

"I told you to stay in your room."

"I was worried," she said.

He looked at the rifle in her hands.

"What were you gonna do with that?"

"I could've shot him," Annie said. "It would've been all over."

"And word would've got out that I ambushed the Gunsmith," Rome said. "That's not what I want to be known for."

Rankin came out.

"What's she doin' here?"

"That's between her and me," Rome said. "Why don't you join the other men and make sure they know what they're supposed to do."

"You're the boss," Rankin said, and strode away.

"What happened with the Gunsmith?" Annie asked.

"Let's go to the room, and I'll tell you."

They started walking to the hotel.

***

As they entered the hotel room, Annie turned to speak to Rome, but he slapped her across the face, backhanded.

"Wha—" she blurted, putting her hand to her face.

"You have to do what I tell you to do," he said, "or you can't be with me. Understood?"

"I—but—y-yes, I understand."

He put his hands out, but as she flinched, he simply gathered her into a hug.

"Then we're fine, right?"

"Y-yes," she said, "we're fine."

He began to undress her . . .

***

Clint couldn't tell whether or not Harry Rome was lying. He would find out on the street in the morning if he was going to face one or two men, or seven. Or, if Ben Vincent appeared on Rome's side, eight.

***

Harry Rome fucked Annie Stark brutally, stripping her naked and then bending her over to take her from behind. He fucked her like she was a whore, which shocked her almost as much as the slap across the face. She thought she had found a man who would take her away from that life, but as he pounded in and out of her from behind, she realized she had been mistaken. There was nothing left but for her to do her job, so she gave herself to the task and as he drove into her, she drove back, and before long the room was filled with the sound of moist flesh-on-flesh. She gave him every indication that she was enjoying their exertions.

Before long she lunged forward, extracting herself from his hold, then pushing him down she mounted him and took him inside. She rode him for as long as she could before he roared and emptied his seed into her . . .

**

Harry Rome stood naked at the window, staring down at the street.

From the bed the naked Annie asked, "So, have you decided what you're going to do?"

"Not quite," he said. "All I know is, only one of us will leave town alive."

Before he slapped her and put her into her place, she might have had something to say. But now she simply laid on her back and waited for him to come back to bed and savage her again.

**

Clint decided to turn in for the night, get some rest, and be ready for whatever came the next day. One man, two, seven or eight, he had his Peacemaker, and his Colt New Line.

Twelve bullets should be plenty.

Chapter Forty-Five

Annie woke the next morning, sore to the bone. The man she thought was going to save her had brutalized her all night. She looked at her rifle, leaning against the wall in the corner, and wondered if she could get to it before he woke up.

"Shit," he said, opening his eyes.

That answered that question.

***

In the lobby Rankin asked Rome, "When do you wanna do this?"

"After breakfast," Rome said. "I hate killing on an empty stomach."

"Where do you wanna eat?"

"As far from the Gunsmith's hotel as possible," Rome said. "I don't want to run into him until I eat."

As they hit the street Rome asked, "Do the men know what to do?"

"They're waitin' for word from you," Rankin assured him.

"That's good."

"What about the girl?" Rankin asked.

"I'm about done with her," Rome said. "You want her?"

"No, thanks."

"Don't you like women?"

"Not skinny women," Rankin said. "I like meat on my girls."

"I'll just get rid of her, then," Rome said. "After breakfast."

***

Clint stayed close to his hotel and ate breakfast at a small restaurant. As well as his holstered Peacemaker, he had his Colt New Line tucked into his belt. He also had his rifle leaning against the table. He was ready for whatever came.

He started his day with steak-and-eggs, and knew it could only go downhill from there.

***

Rome and Rankin finished their breakfast and went out onto the street. Across the way they saw the other five men, leaning and watching.

"Now what?" Rankin asked.

"Now we wait."

"Are you gonna face Adams alone?" Rankin asked.

"That was my intention," Rome said, "but now I don't think I can take him. And if I let him kill me, it's the end of The Six."

"And when this is over, I'll be one of The Six, right?" Rankin asked.

"That's right."

"Then we'll take him together," Rankin said. "It's the only way."

"Okay."

Rankin looked across the street.

"And what about them?"

"We might as well use them, too," Rome said. "Put them on either side of the street, tell them not to fire until we do."

"Right."

***

Clint came out of the café and saw Rome and Rankin in the street. He also saw the other men on both sides of the street.

Apparently, Rome decided he needed the help, after all.

Clint stepped into the street.

"Looks like you decided you need help."

"Well," Rome said, "you *are* the Gunsmith."

"Yes, I am."

Rome looked around, didn't see anyone else on the street but his men.

"You actually did come for me alone," he said.

"That's right."

"Can you see now how foolish that was?"

"I was foolish to think you'd be a man who fought his own battles," Clint said.

"Well," Rome said, "that was my intention, but when I gave it some thought I knew I'd never take the Gunsmith. Not alone, anyway. Standing alone, that's a fool's decision."

"What about you, Rankin?" Clint asked. "You want to try me?"

"I always have," Rankin said, "but not today."

"Today's *my* day," Rome said, "the start of a new Six. I just have to get past you, Adams, no matter how I have to do it."

Clint looked around.

"You have enough guns behind you," Clint said, "but you must know that, no matter what, I'll kill you first." He looked at Rankin. "And you second."

Clint dropped his rifle to the ground, leaving both hands empty to draw his pistols.

"Then I guess we better get to it," Harry Rome said.

Chapter Forty-Six

Rome and Rankin stepped away from each other, putting about five feet between them.

"That's far enough," Clint said.

The other five men stepped into the street. Clint kept his eyes on Rankin. He was the one who was going to call the play.

As he watched, Rankin went for his gun. At his first move, the others followed.

As Clint shot Rankin, he heard a show from above. Rome spun around as a bullet struck him. Annie fired again from her hotel window, putting a second bullet into him, this time in his chest.

The other five men stopped for a moment, looking up at the hotel window. Before they could move, Ben Vincent stepped out of a doorway behind them and began to fire. Clint also fired, and the five men weren't sure which way to turn. By the time they decided they were dancing in the street as lead drove into them from three directions.

When it was over, Clint stood with both his guns in his hands. He tucked the New Line into his belt and reloaded the Peacemaker, just in case.

Annie Stark came out the front door of the hotel, carrying her rifle.

Ben Vincent crossed from the other side of the street, holstering his gun.

"I wondered where you got to," Clint said.

"I thought it was best to stay out of sight until the right time came."

"And you?" Clint asked Annie.

"Rome turned out to not be the man I thought he was," she said. "I don't know where I'll go now, but it'll be without him."

"I'm glad to see you both, then," Clint said.

Vincent turned and looked at the man who was approaching them.

"What's the sheriff's part?" Vincent asked.

"He'll keep you in custody until I'm ready to leave," Clint said. "As I promised, I'll speak at your trial."

When the sheriff reached them, Vincent unholstered his gun and held it out to him.

"The Six are gone?" the lawman asked, accepting the gun.

"They are."

The lawman looked at Annie.

"And her?"

"She wasn't part of it," Clint said.

The sheriff nodded and started walking Ben Vincent to his office.

"What will you do now?" Annie asked.

"Send a telegram to the governors of Texas and New Mexico, telling them the job is done."

"Then what?"

"I'll have to take Ben to the Capital. He'll stand trial with Reese, Patch and Kingman, if he's still alive."

"But not me?"

"As you said," Clint said, "you don't know where you're going, but it won't be with them."

She nodded, turned and walked away, her shoulders slumped.

Clint looked around as men chosen by the sheriff began to clean the street. He would leave town with Vincent come morning, happy to leave the place—and The Six—behind him.

Coming Soon!

THE GUNSMITH
476
DEADLY DELIVERY

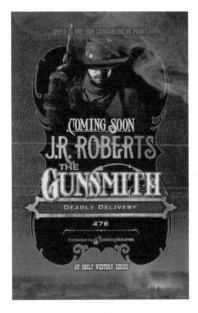

**For more information
visit:** www.SpeakingVolumes.us

On Sale Now!

THE GUNSMITH *series*
Books 430 – 474

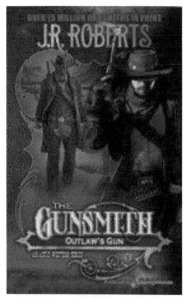

For more information
visit: www.SpeakingVolumes.us

On Sale Now!

THE GUNSMITH GIANT *series*

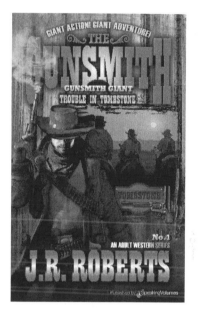

**For more information
visit:** www.SpeakingVolumes.us

On Sale Now!

Lady Gunsmith *series*
Books 1 - 9
Roxy Doyle and the Lady Executioner

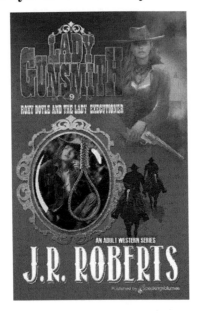

For more information
visit: www.SpeakingVolumes.us

On Sale Now!

TALBOT ROPER NOVELS
by
ROBERT J. RANDISI

**For more information
visit:** <u>www.SpeakingVolumes.us</u>

On Sale Now!

Award-Winning Author
Robert J. Randisi (J.R. Roberts)

For more information
visit:

Sign up for free and bargain books

Join the Speaking Volumes mailing list

Text

ILOVEBOOKS

to 22828 to get started.

Message and data rates may apply

25502538R00125